VILLAINS

IT'S SAVAGE SEASON

THE COLDEST KILLER SINCE KALI
- C. WASH, VP

T. STYLES

NATIONAL BESTSELLING AUTHOR OF *RAUNCHY*

2   By T. STYLES

4   By T. STYLES

WWW.THECARTELPUBLICATIONS.COM

VILLAINS: IT'S SAVAGE SEASON   5

Villains: It's Savage Season

By

T. Styles

By T. STYLES

Library of Congress Control Number: 2018933916

ISBN 10: 1945240253

ISBN 13: 978-1945240256

Cover Design: Davida Baldwin

www.oddballdsgn.com

www.thecartelpublications.com
First Edition
Printed in the United States of America

What's Up Fam,

I just wanna jump right in and tell you how much I truly enjoyed the latest tale that was birthed from the incredibly creative twisted mind of T. Styles. This damn VILLAINS book had me on the edge of my seat!

I done found a dude that is more calculating and murderous than some of T. Styles' worst killers. I swear, Kanati is now in my top 5 of her characters!

So without further adieu I will wrap this little note to you up so that you can dive head first into this one. Order a pizza for the fam and put your phone on airplane mode cuz you not gonna wanna be disturbed!

With that being said, keeping in line with tradition, we want to give respect to a vet or trailblazer paving the way. In this novel, we would like to recognize:

GABOUREY SIDIBE

Gabourey Sidibe is an Academy Award nominated actress and author. We first fell in love with her amazing talent in the movie, "Precious" for which she

By T. STYLES

earned her Oscar nod. More recently she has been on the very successful TV show, "Empire" and now she has penned her own novel. Her book is called, "This Is Just My Face: Try Not To Stare". It's a Gabby's hard-hitting memoir on, "friendship, depression, celebrity, haters, fashion, race and weight. So make sure you add this one to your must read list!

Aight, get to it. I'll catch you in the next book.

Be Easy!

Charisse "C. Wash" Washington
Vice President
The Cartel Publications
www.thecartelpublications.com
www.facebook.com/publishercwash
Instagram: publishercwash
www.twitter.com/cartelbooks
www.facebook.com/cartelpublications
Follow us on Instagram: Cartelpublications
#CartelPublications
#UrbanFiction
#PrayForCeCe
#GaboureySidibe

CARTEL URBAN CINEMA'S WEB SERIES

BMORE CHICKS

@ Pink Crystal Inn

NOW AVAILABLE:

Via

YOUTUBE

And

DVD

(Season 2 Coming Summer 2018)

www.youtube.com/user/tstyles74

www.cartelurbancinema.com

www.thecartelpublications.com

By T. STYLES

#Villains

12   By T. STYLES

When this story ends I'll be a dead man.

Don't bother rushing the journey. This isn't some scheme to get you to hear every gory detail of my life either.

Simply put, this is the truth.

My truth.

Many events have happened that brought me to the end of my life. Some as vivid as this bleeding wound on my body. While other events seem to have gotten blurred in my mind with the passage of time.

But if you ask me my biggest regret it's this...I should have never judged the book by its cover the day I met him.

Use my life as a message.

Goodbye.

PROLOGUE

Death was near.

Before it's presence The Sleeping Man rested peacefully in bed until he was jolted heavily by the sound of a soft whistle. A whistle that at first may have seemed pleasant and no big deal to the average person. But he heard tales of the sound in the past and knew that to some trap niggas it meant death.

Slowly he pushed the covers back and immediately a thick chill overcame his body. And now that his breath had quickened every time he exhaled, a puff of cold air rolled from his nostrils and floated above before disappearing into the ether.

He hadn't turned the temperature so low so who had?

Whistle.

Startled again, he grabbed the sheet and sat on the edge of the bed. His bare toes pressed into the cool hardwood floor.

Whistle.

With his thoughts choppy, he realized that in his angst he hadn't awakened his beloved to warn her of

By T. STYLES

their fate. But when he reached for her he realized her space was empty.

What was happening?

Where was she?

Slowly he rose and approached the window, the floor creaked softly with his weighty steps. Taking a deep breath, he pushed the thick velvet red curtains to the side and peered out the window. His warm breath caressed the pane, temporarily covering his view with a thick fog. Taking a strong hand he wiped it harshly and what he saw caused him to shiver.

Standing on the roof of his green Mercedes Benz was The Killer. His long curly hair was tamed at the root with a black bandana but still blew in the wind.

He wasn't alone.

On top of the silver Aston Martin to the right was another man and on top of the white Range Rover to the left of The Killer was yet another.

Holding a knife, The Killer smiled when he saw The Sleeping Man's face from the window.

"Found you," The Killer yelled. "I hope you made your peace."

CHAPTER ONE

LAWRENCE "LAW" HIGHTOWER

SOME YEARS EARLIER

Law stood in the middle of his father's living room with a sly grin on his face. The soft glow from the heritage hand cut crystal chandelier above him appeared out of place for the gory scene before him. Especially since he was watching Sylvia slam the blade of a knife as quickly as possible between her small brown fingers, hoping to prevent getting cut.

Spoiled corrupt, Law got off on the game and luckily she granted him the honor of seeing her do this many times before. She paid dearly for her services too. Sylvia was even one finger short on her left hand due to participating in the vicious sport and yet the lure of money was too much for the young coke addict to resist.

"Faster!" Law said licking his lips as he watched her slam the knife quicker, each time jabbing into the black cutting board atop the twenty thousand dollar table. "You not moving quick enough for me! I ain't paying you if you not making this shit real."

By T. STYLES

Hearing his request she went faster, hoping to eventually please the lunatic who was paying her a pittance.

In the audience were his friends who didn't miss a chance to freeload off the luxurious lifestyle Jimmy, Law's father, provided. A serial strip club owner in Baltimore city, Jimmy made a living off the best dancers money could by. And with his top of the line security, thug entrepreneurs felt safe in his space so they rewarded him with their business.

Law's friends included Moozy, an overweight twenty something dude with a severe greed and acne problem. And Leather Face who they nicked named L.F., after he burned himself during a grease fire while frying chicken. A moniker that stayed with him so long that those who didn't know him before the event weren't aware that his real name was Daniel.

Finally there was Petey, who at 5'6 was much shorter than his friends. But what he lacked in height he made up for in extreme intelligence. Conniving to the core, Petey could foresee an enemy's next move, which made him invaluable since Law stayed with the drama in the streets.

To some it may appear that the quartet was an odd grouping but there was a method to Law's madness.

At 6'2 with a body to die for and looks to match, his rag tag group of friends made him shine even brighter. He had money, women dropping to their knees to be with him and clout but he wanted total adoration from everyone in Baltimore. Of course the city liked him, not because he earned it, but because of his lineage.

At twenty-six years old Law was given the world but still that wasn't enough. There was always a nagging sensation to get and have more. The growing pill business he was building in the city gave him riches but he always felt like something was missing. Petey said it was the love of a woman. But Law said no woman could ever tame him. He believed he thrived on danger.

And adventure by honorable mention.

"Oww!" Sylvia suddenly screamed out. While stabbing the knife through the spaces of her fingers, she severed a digit yet again. Dropping the knife to the white expensive carpet, dousing it with blood, she quickly leapt to her feet. "It's gonna come off!" She cried wide eyes twirling around her sockets. "It's gonna come off!" The finger was already swinging off like the pendulum on a grandfather clock.

Law laughed hysterically, pointing at her with a stiff long finger. "That bitch dangling!" He slapped L.F. on the shoulder. "Look, man!"

L.F. looked and chuckled once, not amused. Especially since he was already deformed and saw no humor in that area.

"I'm gonna die!" Sylvia cried. "I'm gonna die and you don't care."

"'Aight, 'aight, you gonna be okay," Law said calming down.

With wide eyes she continued to hold her severed digit, which was hanging on by a few tendons. "I'm gonna lose it and you don't care! You don't fucking care!"

Now she was blowing his high. Annoyed as fuck, he shook his head, tiring already of her whining. Wanting her out of his house he slammed a hand on Moozy's beefy shoulder. Moozy may have been eyeing the game a little while it was in session but most of his focus was on the bag of Cheetos in one hand and the plain Lays potato chips in the other, claiming that together they tasted better than fresh pussy.

Most niggas disagreed.

"Aye, get up, Moo and take her ass to the hospital."

He frowned. "But I was eating my —"

Law slapped the bags out of his lap and clenched his fists. Chip remnants flew up into the air and feathered downward all over his father's ten thousand dollar couch and floor. "Get yah ass up and take her to the hospital. Don't make me ask again, my nigga."

Realizing he pushed Law too far Moozy stood up and followed Sylvia who was already rushing toward the exit. Before she left, while holding her finger, she turned to Law and said, "But what about my money?"

Law ran his hand down his cheek and crossed his arms over his chest. "I'll get that to you later." He nodded. "Get up out of here and see about that finger. You don't wanna lose it."

She frowned. "But you said you were gonna pay me the last time."

"Yo, get the fuck up out my face, bitch!" He paused. "You didn't even do it right."

When they walked out, Vanessa, Law's only female friend strutted inside, closing the door behind her. Her bone straight red wig ran down her back and stopped at the tip of her fat ass. She was the only one of Law's exes who got over him dogging her out and because of it he allowed her to hang with them from time to time. Provided the city knew that they were only friends, nothing more or less. Truth be told, if he were being honest, her company wasn't too terrible for him to endure. Besides, the red bone was sexy to look at, of that there was no doubt.

"Man, why you keep fucking with that girl?" Vanessa asked flopping on the sofa, knocking chips and Cheetos out the way. "She gonna get back at your ass. Mark my words." She opened her brown Luis Vuitton Neverfull purse.

"I keep telling him that one day he gonna pay for all the foul ass shit he do to niggas." Petey said, while playing chess on his cell phone. "But he don't listen." He shrugged. "Guess every man has to learn for himself."

Law walked up to him. "You sound dumb as fuck."

Petey shook his head and chuckled. "Yeah, aight."

"Okay," Law continued, "Answer me this, Pete. What nigga alive time enough for me? I'll wait."

Petey shrugged. "I don't know his name." He pointed at him. "But he's out there. Trust me."

"Fuck all that, yah going to the party?" Vanessa asked, smoothing strawberry Chapstick on her lips, before dropping it back into her purse. "Because I heard it's gonna be like that tonight. Might even get me a man."

Law frowned at her and then cleared his throat when she caught his jealous gaze. "Well I'm tired of parties," Law said. "You meet the same broads week after week." He continued and gripped his dick for the reposition. "I'm tired of fucking road kill." He walked up to Vanessa. "So you sure you going?"

"Yes but don't worry." She sat back and crossed her legs. "If I do I ain't gonna be around you and the rest of these ugly ass niggas up in here," she joked.

"You calling my friends ugly?" Law said, although knowing she was speaking gospel. "How you sound?"

"I ain't paying her no mind," Petey said. "It's about the dick," he gripped himself, "not the looks." He winked.

"Whatever, nigga." She got up and switched toward the window when she saw movement outside from afar. The moment she pushed the cream chiffon curtains to the side she smiled. Law, L.F. and Petey wondered why. "What you need to be doing is bringing some new faces with you. Maybe you can meet some new bitches then." From her view she could see Kanati Dawson doing pull-ups in a tree using the branch. "Bring Kanati's fine ass." She turned her head to look at Law. "He'll make the ugliest of your bunch look snackable." She looked out the window again. "That's for sure." She licked her lips.

Kanati lie on the floor in the living room of the guesthouse he stayed in behind Jimmy's mansion. He had just finished doing pull-ups on the tree and now was doing sit-ups in the house. Mixed with Navaho Indian and African American respectfully, he definitely had an appeal women found alluring.

And yet he belonged to only one.

Sunni Hamden.

A resident of a reservation in Arizona, she was waiting for him to return home to her in a day. Although he didn't like being away from her, Kanati was only in Maryland because Jimmy had recently bought horses and had no idea on how to raise them. And Kanati, who grew up around them all of his life, needed the money to support his family. Besides, just like with over eighty percent of all Indian reservations in America, he and his family lived in extreme poverty and so he welcomed the opportunity to make good money.

By working for Jimmy for just three months, he had managed to raise over $20,000 because Jimmy was a big tipper. Most of the money Kanati earned would be used to fix up the living conditions on the reservation while the other funds would be used to propose to Sunni when the time was right.

He always had a plan and his loyalty was the reason many loved him.

"I do miss you," Sunni said as she spoke to him from the cell phone, which was on speaker next to where he was doing sit-ups. "These people here are so boring and—"

"But they're family, Sunni," he said passionately. "And it makes me sad that you don't love your home and people as much as I do."

"It's not like that." She sighed. "It's just that I need more," Sunni said seriously. "I need an adventure and I need a life. I wish you could understand that."

KNOCK! KNOCK! KNOCK!

"I have to go," Kanati stood up and grabbed his towel off the chair. "I'll see you tomorrow." He ended the call and wiped the sweat off his face and tossed the towel over his bare shoulder.

When Kanati opened the door, with Law in the lead, he, Petey, L.F. and Vanessa moved inside without an invitation. Law was rude as fuck as usual as he pushed through the crib in authority mode. In Law's mind the house was his father's even if Kanati lived there for the time being.

Law's visit was unusual to say the least. Kanati had seen him around the mansion but for the most part he never spoke to him preferring instead to treat Kanati like a disrespected third world citizen. So Kanati wondered what spawned the change?

Putting a firm hand on Kanati's shoulder Law said, "What up, Chief?" He led Kanati further into the small house and into the living room.

"Hey, Law," Kanati nodded. "What's up with you? I was just working out. Did Jimmy need something?" He smiled.

In fact Kanati was rarely seen without a smile and because of it he exuded a man who was always happy. This in turn irritated Law to no end.

Fuck he had to be happy for? He was broke. To hear Law tell it.

"What you just say you doing?" Law said frowning. "I ain't hear you."

Kanati, confused, repeated his statement. "I said I was working out."

"What?" Law screamed louder. "I ain't hear you."

"I said I was working out."

"What?" Law repeated before finally falling out laughing at his own juvenile humor.

"Leave the man alone and stop playing," Vanessa said before tugging Kanati's hand and pulling him down to the sofa. When Kanati was seated she placed her hand on his thigh and scooted a little closer. There was no room between them. Even his sweat smelled sweet. "Well the working out is paying off," she said licking her lips. "That's for sure."

Law frowned again. "Stop acting like a slut."

"Well he is fine," she continued eyeing him again.

But Kanati looked away from her. Vanessa was beautiful but he didn't know who she was with and didn't want any of them thinking he was putting moves on her. "Thank you. I appreciate—"

"Fuck all that," Law said with L.F. standing behind him, staring down at Kanati like they owned him. "What you doing tonight? It ain't like you got a life so it shouldn't really be nothing."

"Actually I was—"

"You coming with us," Law said cutting him off, hands clutched in front of him, his head tilted slightly to the side.

Kanati smiled again and shook his head softly from left to right. "Nah, it's my last day and —"

"Listen, I'm not taking no for an answer." Law paused. "So say yes or I'm going to be hounding you all night."

Kanati shook his head. He wasn't interested in doing anything with Law but at the same time didn't want to be rude either. At the end of the day Law was the boss's son and this was a delicate matter. "It's just that I'm flying home tomorrow and —"

"You might as well say yes, nigga," L.F. added to the conversation. "You can go to sleep on the plane."

Kanati looked up at Law and took a deep breath. It was obvious that he had intentions on pestering him all night. He might as well agree and be done with it once and for all. "Okay, maybe I can hang out for a little while."

"Okay?" Law repeated, as if he didn't press him harder than a convict fresh out of jail trying to get some pussy. "You really rolling with us?"

"Yes." Kanati repeated, smiling again. "I'll —"

"Who this?" Petey asked walking back into the living room although no one realized he was gone until that moment. He went searching into the man's house and found gold.

A framed photo of a stunning woman.

"She's, she's my girlfriend." Kanati moved uneasily in his seat. Partially because he didn't know he had been in his bedroom. "Well, she'll be my fiancé when I ask for her hand."

"Fuck all that," Law said, snatching the picture from Petey without looking at it. "Why you bring this out here anyway?" He asked Petey. "We don't want my man thinking about her tonight since he 'bout to fuck some real…"

Finally his gaze fell on the photo and time stopped. Moving it closer to his face he was thrown off by the woman's beauty. In his young ass life, he'd never seen a bitch bad as her and yet she was doing nothing erotic. Sunni was simply sitting on a tree swing wearing all white as her long hair danced in the wind around her angelic face, causing it to freeze in time.

He had to have her.

"You 'aight, man?" Petey asked, believing Law was doing too much with the photo.

"Oh, yeah," Law looked at Kanati and cleared his throat. "You, you said this your girl?"

"Yes." Kanati smiled again.

"Wow," Law continued. "She's everything." He put the photo on the table, before stealing one last glance. Slapping his hands together once he said, "Well you one lucky nigga that's for sure." He nodded and looked down at the picture again. His niggas cleared their throats, embarrassed for Kanati. "Listen, I'll be back later to scoop you and Vanessa gonna braid you up. Don't get me wrong, in Arizona it may be the move but out here you might look too feminine for these bitches."

For the first time Kanati frowned.

"Ain't nothing wrong with his hair," Vanessa said touching it. "I actually think it's sexy all wild and shit."

"Still, braid it up like the fuck I said," Law snapped.

"'Aight, boy!" She yelled rolling her eyes. "Calm down!"

Law, L.F. and Petey walked out the door but Vanessa hung back a little to examine Kanati closer, as if sensing something deeper to the smile he'd always worn.

To the untrained eye someone would see the curly black hair that ran down his back and his wide eyes and deem him to be soft but she wondered if they'd be wrong.

"Why you always smiling, Kanati?" She paused. "Since you've been working here I've never seen you angry."

He looked down and then back at her. "I smile because it keeps the rage away."

"And what happens when you get angry?"

"I'll see you tonight." He got up and walked away.

By T. STYLES

CHAPTER TWO

LAW

Law was cruising down the street in his black BMW with Petey in the passenger seat playing Scrabble on his cell phone. Kanati and L.F. were in the back riding along as Law blasted *XXXTentacion* from his speakers.

Although Law was in route to the party he still couldn't believe a woman he never met mesmerized him. It was amazing that Sunni was all he could think about. The entire ride he plotted in his mind what needed to happen to get her but he was coming up short. Besides, the woman was on the other side of the country.

"Vanessa and Moo said they already there," L.F. said while texting on his phone. "Just waiting on us."

Law nodded and then looked at Kanati through the rear view mirror. "You good back there, Chief?"

"Yep," he smiled and nodded before looking down at the clothes Law bought him to look the part of a drug dealer's minion.

Although Kanati preferred his signature blue jeans, white t-shirt or wifebeater, tonight he was wearing black designer jeans and a black Gucci long sleeve shirt. His curly hair was braided into six cornrows that ran down his back. He looked like a model.

Despite his evil ways Law was no slouch on the evening either. Sporting blue jeans and a red Balenciaga t-shirt, his hair was recently shaped up and fresh.

They were almost at the club when suddenly they ran over a bump in the road, which jolted the car upwards and then downward roughly. Slowly Law reduced the speed of his ride, which was now driving wobbly. Angry he slapped the steering wheel. "Fuck!" He looked at his friends. "I think the tire just blew!"

Petey looked over at him and shrugged. "So. Just change it." He focused back on his game. "It ain't hard."

"Nigga, I left the jack at the barber shop today. Remember?" He paused. "I knew I was gonna forget it there. Should've never let him use it."

"Left the jack at the barber shop for fucking what?" L.F. chimed in from the backseat, offering no resolution. "What kind of sense does that make?"

"Luther needed it and —" he took a deep breath. "You know what, it doesn't even matter. It's not in the trunk."

L.F. leaned forward. "Then what we gonna do?" He looked at Petey and then back at Law as if the world was about to end. "Because we can't lift the car without the jack. We gonna be late." He fell back into the seat roughly.

Law frowned. "How you sound? All you gonna do is bang the same fat bitch you did last week." He shook his head. "Now calm down so I can think. You not missing out on nothing anyway."

L.F. glared when he wasn't looking.

"I'll change it," Kanati said calmly.

"Ain't you listening?" Law asked while turning around to look at him. "We don't have a jack."

"I can still do it." He said confidently. "Just need one person to pull the tire off and put the new one on while I hold it up."

Law laughed. "So you expect me to believe you can lift this bitch up?"

Silence.

L.F. grinned, happy about the possibility of getting to the party. "'Aight, I'll play along." He shrugged and tapped Kanati's chest with the back of his hand. "Let's go."

"Can you pop the trunk?" Kanati asked Law. "I just need the lug wrench and the tire. You got them right?"

Law nodded and complied. They got out, closed the car doors, leaving Petey and Law alone.

"Should we get out?" Petey asked.

"Nah. Fuck him."

After a few seconds the car raised a little and Law and Petey looked at them through the back window. After discovering that Kanati did exactly what he said he would do, Petey faced the front again and continued to play his game. "Something's up with that nigga."

"Whatever." Law smirked. "The only thing he got going on is that bitch. And he not 'bout to have her when I'm done."

Petey put his phone down and looked over at him. Taking a deep breath he ran his hands down his face and then pressed them together in a praying motion. "Please leave that woman alone, man. I'm begging you. Yes she's bad. Yes she's finer than anything we've seen in a long time. But she's not yours."

Law smiled. "Why you acting so scared?"

"Because fucking with her feels dangerous." He paused. "I can't explain it." He looked back at Kanati who was still holding the car up.

Law laughed again and looked out the driver's side window at the passing vehicles. In his mind Petey

By T. STYLES

could talk all he wanted but he was not moving from his position. The woman in the photo would be playing host to his dick before the year's end. He would stake his life on it. "Yeah, whatever." He waved him off.

"All you see is the surface of niggas," Petey continued. "And you think each man is made up the same. Well I'm telling you right now that, that dude is trouble." He pointed toward the back.

"I guess we gonna find out then huh?" He rubbed his hands together.

Petey lifted his phone and continued to play. "Your funeral."

After some time, the tire was changed and Kanati placed the ruptured one in the trunk, closing it afterwards. Kanati and L.F. walked back to the car. Although L.F. crawled inside, Kanati stayed outside and strutted up to the driver's side window.

"Listen, I'm gonna call it a night," Kanati said. He looked toward the back of the BMW. "Your tire should be good enough to get you there but you have to be careful driving."

"But I wanted to introduce you to the city," Law frowned. "I thought you were rolling. That's what you said anyway."

"I'm sure I'll get a chance to meet the city. I'm coming back next month." He paused and tapped the top of the car once, stepping back. "But I have an early flight and to be honest I'm already beat." He shook Law's hand. "Thank your friend for doing my braids though."

Law nodded and slowly looked forward. The pause of silence was so long that everyone wondered what he was about to say. Simply put, he wasn't a man who was use to not getting his way so Petey knew trouble was near. "You know what," Law looked at Kanati. "I'm coming with you."

L.F. frowned while Petey shook his head slowly from left to right, dropping his cell phone in his lap. This was truly the worst-case scenario.

"Petey, you drive." Law got out and closed the door. "Me and my man gonna catch an Uber and I'm going with him to Arizona."

"What you doing, man?" Petey whispered, not being able to go into more detail for fear Kanati would pick up on Law's plans. He knew Law was on some larceny shit as it pertained to Kanati's girl and he was trying to save him the trouble. "People waiting on you at the club."

"I'm tired of doing the same shit in Bmore." He put a hand on Kanati's shoulder. "I want the Chief to show me his city." He looked at Kanati. "What you say? You up for that, man?"

Law walked down the aisle of the plane holding his stomach. He had thrown up so much he smelled of vomit and felt light headed as he moved. When he finally made it back to his seat he looked over at Kanati who was sitting by the window looking out of it calmly. It was as if they were on two different flights and Kanati didn't feel the turbulence. Despite the rocking tin can the clouds looked like the center of ice cubes against the artic blue sky.

In all the beauty, Law couldn't see it. His heart was black as hate. Plopping in his seat he stared at Kanati. Kanati's face held a peace that he wanted for himself but felt he'd never have. "How can you take this trip back to back?" Law asked, holding his queasy stomach. The terrain over the mountains had his guts rocking. "It's been jumping for hours."

Kanati smiled and looked back out the window. "Flying is the closest you can get to heaven." He shrugged. "And I love it."

Law grinned because he could think of some other ways to get a nigga to heaven if he applied himself. "Whatever the fuck," he said waving his hand at Kanati. A disrespectful bundle of mess. "I'm a city nigga and this ain't me. I prefer the land."

Two hours later they were in a truck driving over dirt while the blue skyline played host to the large gray mountains. As the trip got longer it was obvious that where they were going was nothing like the tourist traps most people visited while in Arizona.

Nah, the reservation was just like the hoods in Baltimore City but grimier, sadder and not as talked about.

Some Native Americans, although the original people, were now plagued with extreme poverty, alcoholism and drugs. It was as if the government was doing all it could to help the indigenous people kill themselves once and for all thereby hiding the dirty memory of how they roughed the entire country.

And it was working.

When they finally came about brown worn out dwellings and structures Law looked over at Kanati.

There were about twenty-two houses that the people built, most of which were leaning over and barely stable. Since they had no running water, due to owning the land but not having the system in place to mine the water, because that was owned by the government, they were forced to go to a well about ten miles off the reservation. "How could you live here?" Law frowned.

Kanati smiled. "You'll see," He said confidently.

Law took a deep breath. "I don't know about all that but listen...I don't wanna go meet your people empty-handed. So what can I bring 'em?" He was really asking what could he bring Sunni but he didn't want the naive fool catching onto his scheme. Everything within time. "I mean, it would be rude not to have something with me right?"

"A sheep." Kanati said confidently. "They'll love it."

Law leaned in. "What?"

"We use them for the wool and the meat. Trust me, my family would appreciate it a lot."

Law felt queasy again just thinking about the concept of eating or skinning the animal. "Well, maybe I can find something else, man. I don't know 'bout looking for no sheep and—"

"If you want to impress my family it doesn't get much better than that." Kanati paused. "Besides, I know a place."

An hour later, after visiting a herder, Law and Kanati arrived at the reservation with two sheep since Law decided to splurge. He didn't understand Native American's traditions but if he was gonna impress Sunni in his opinion he had to go all out.

The moment Kanati stepped off the pick up truck a hoard of people ran up to him with cheers and hugs. Wow. When Law saw the reception Kanati was getting he finally got what Kanati meant when he said, "You'll see."

Kanati was embraced in so much love and Law wondered how they could respect a man who in his opinion appeared soft. It was as if he were some sort of God. Similar to how he was in Baltimore but different.

After some time, finally the crowd opened through the middle. Suddenly a woman no taller than five feet appeared wearing a purple and gold shimmering muumuu. The strands of her hair shined like pure silver and the lines on her soft face were etched to perfection, like rows on the bark of an oak tree.

Slowly she moved toward Kanati and he lowered his upper body so she could touch his face gently. In the ancient Na-Dene' tongue that only Kanati, Sunni and she could speak on the reservation, she said, "You're home." She paused. "I missed you so much, Kanati." She smiled and kissed both of his cheeks. "It seemed like forever."

"I missed you too, Nanni."

She smiled and touched him again. But when she released Kanati something shook her core and she glared in Law's direction. His energy felt like death. Kanati was too busy hugging other family and friends to notice the dark exchange. At eighty years old, it was as if the woman knew his foul intentions. Like his bad deeds were written on his face and she could read his mind.

Finally Sunni stepped up to Kanati and it was the moment Law was waiting for. *Wow.* He thought. Her pictures didn't do her justice and he would never trust the validity of a photograph ever again. Wearing a white dress with small straps her inky black hair poured over her frame like a mink fur.

She was breathtaking.

Walking up to her Kanati said, "Sunni, how I missed you."

She smiled and kissed him passionately before Law cleared his throat. Not being able to take much more.

Besides, in Law's firm opinion she belonged to him. She just didn't know it yet. The suspense was killing him and rudeness took over. Causing the man to break up the exchange he was making with his woman.

And Kanati, taking the hint that Law wanted to meet the family, separated from his love and walked over to him. "Family, I want you all to meet Law. He's the son of the man who allowed me to earn a living at his home. We all should feel grateful for his presence."

Filled with gratitude every one of the members of the reservation happily shook Law's hand. For a brief moment Law felt like the devil himself knowing his intentions were anything but admirable. Still, it was Sunni who he came to meet and anybody else could kill themselves.

So when she moved to him he quickly embraced her hand and held it longer than need be. When Nanni touched her arm, she snatched away from him and looked at the pick up truck behind them. "I see you came bearing gifts." She said to Law. "Although I wish Kanati would've said to bring something else."

Law wondered if she was embarrassed about the primitive gift and he made mental notes. Maybe she was a hustler's wife material after all. He knew he should've stuck with his original idea and bought a couple of bottles instead. "I was gonna get some champagne." He smiled. "But Kanati said it would be a good idea to get the goats."

"Sheep," Kanati laughed. "They are sheep."

"Yeah...sheep," Law said looking at her more intensely than ever. Law's disrespect was so bad a group of men about Kanati's age left the scene, none wanting to meet him.

"Then what are we waiting on?" She asked. "Let us feast!" Her excitement caused everyone to break out into cheer.

As Kanati's family escorted Law further onto the reservation, his grandmother walked up to Kanati again. In her native tongue she spoke to him from deep inside. "So the time has come." She said sadly. "And although I prayed it never would...still...here we are."

"What you mean?"

"You have brought the devil himself to our home. And it will mean the end of everything sacred." With a lowered head she walked away leaving him confused.

A purple black sky covered the reservation bringing out stars so bright they resembled millions of tiny flashlights shining back to earth. A Hogan, a traditional Navajo structure, which was once originally built to live in, was now filled with food and drinks for the celebration. Outside of the dwelling was a fire where tasty meat sat on a spit over it which was turned every so often by the chefs. Kanati's family, mostly drunk at this point, laughed and enjoyed each other's company despite it now being well into the night.

Feeling on top of the world, Kanati who had been looking for Law finally found him outside the Hogan watching Sunni dance. Smiling proudly, Kanati placed his hand on his shoulder, which startled him at first. "I been looking all over for you." Kanati said. "You good?"

"Perfect." Law nodded at him. "But I can see why you love it here." Law looked up at the sky and back at Sunni. "Feels like peace."

Kanati smiled. "It is. Heaven on earth."

Law nodded again and tried desperately not to clock the man's woman. But he couldn't take his eyes off of her if he tried. She was just that fucking bad. "So, uh, what you do around here, Chief?"

"The rodeo is a big thing which is how I know about horses." Kanati said stuffing his hands into his pockets. "Other than that I'm all about family. In our culture the plan was to originally learn from the whites and then come back and teach our people." He sighed. "But most of them don't want to learn anymore. Me, Nanni and Sunni are the only ones who even speak the language."

"I'm sorry, man." Law said. "I—"

"Hold up." When Kanati saw Sunni abruptly walk away like something was wrong he said, "I'll be right back. Make yourself at home."

Worried, Kanati followed her to her small house on the reservation where she sat on a plastic white chair outside her door. The orange glow from the flames across the way caused her skin to sparkle. "What's wrong, Sunni?" He sat next to her. "You look upset."

She gazed at him, her eyes tearing up now resembling marbles. "I'm unhappy." She sighed. "Still. And it's like it hit me all at once."

Having heard this before he touched her hand. "I know but I promise I'm trying to make the life you want." He squeezed softly. "I already earned $20,000 to fix up the reservation and to give you the life you deserve. Just hang in there with me while I build a little more." He paused. "Please."

"But I want more now, Kanati! Not then!" She shook out of his hold. "And I'm ready to do anything for it!"

He leaned in. "What does that mean?"

Silence.

"Sunni, what does that mean?"

"You already know," she said. "I mean can you really take care of me?"

He shook his head. "I hate when you talk like this." He paused. "It makes you sound shallow."

"Your dream is to build up the reservation but my dream is to move away from it. And if that makes me shallow then so be it. I mean, why can't we move to Maryland or —"

"No." He shook his head from left to right quickly. "The nature there is too corrupt. Plus I can't leave everybody else here." He paused. "I promise, you'll come to love the life I'm building for us when we finish here. Just trust me."

"But what if I don't?" She looked at him as her eyes continued to twinkle from the fire some ways ahead. "Then what?"

"Sunni, what do you want from me?"

She kissed his lips. "Everything and more." She exhaled. "Please forgive me." She got up and walked away leaving him confused by her apology.

Later that night Sunni was brushing her long black hair in her house when Law walked into her bedroom. Uninvited. She smiled when she saw him through her mirror staring at her as if she were a piece of meat. The house was very tiny and looked as if it could be pushed over with a little pressure and still she made it feminine.

"What took you so long?" She asked, as if she knew him. "I've been waiting forever."

He took one step closer, somewhat confused. "What you mean?"

She giggled softly. "I knew you would come."

He lowered his brow. "You mean you knew I would come tonight?" He pointed at himself.

"No. I knew you would come into my life." She placed her brush down and turned to face him. "Just didn't know it would take so long."

He grinned, never expecting to be able to connect with her so easily. The plan was to come in and tell her all the reasons she should bounce with him but this was better. "Is that why you left the door unlocked?"

"Of course." She paused. "You've been watching me all night. And you seemed like the type who would take liberties that weren't granted to you first."

He walked up to her and for a second just stared at her beauty. Her smooth brown skin. Her long black hair. Her wide eyes, tiny nose and little lips. She looked like a doll. "You're the most beautiful thing I've ever seen. Period."

"Thank you." She placed a long strand of her hair behind her ear. "And still I must know, how much are you willing to pay for me?" She asked as she stood up.

Arrogantly he shrugged. "I'ma be straight, ma, money ain't a thing where I'm from. If there's a price I can pay it." He paused. "The only question is are you rolling with me or not?"

She giggled. "I can tell you have financial means but I'm not speaking of that either." She paused. "If I go with you, the cost will be more than even money can buy."

He laughed, thinking the woman a fool. "I know you not talking about Kanati." He pointed behind him.

"The nigga's soft and if he cared about you he would've never brought me here. I been talking about you all night."

"You haven't answered the question."

"You know what," he extended his hand and she accepted, placing her palm into his. "I promise you this, if you come with me I will pay whatever price it costs to keep you. Even if it means war."

That was the answer she was seeking.

Kanati was in his house sleep when loud fighting outside his bedroom window suddenly awakened him from his slumber. Sliding on his jeans with no shirt he went outside to examine the situation. Under the ice blue morning sky he saw his brother by another mother, who was a severe drunk, fist fighting his best friend. Blood covered their frames and Kanati rushed to them to quickly break it up. After all, they once got into a fight so bad that guns were brought into the mix, causing another cousin of Kanati's to be shot in the chin.

When he was upon them he pushed them apart roughly. "What's going on this time?" Kanati asked before rubbing his eyes and yawning. "Fuck is up with yah? Huh? Don't you realize it's early in the morning?"

"He pissed all over my living room floor!" Kanati's brother, Paco, yelled pointing at his friend. "That's what's wrong with me."

"I did not!" His friend yelled. "He peed himself when—"

Suddenly Kanati's attention was diverted when he glanced over and saw Sunni's front door swinging back and forth every time a warm breeze blew. At that moment his brother and his friend were no longer of importance. The niggas were dumb anyway. Confused he ran toward her house to investigate. Standing in the doorway he yelled, "Sunni, you in there?" He paused and looked inside from where he stood. "Sunni, are you—"

"She gone," Paco said with one hand on the wall of her house and the other on his gut as he vomited into the clay colored dirt. "Ain't no need in you going in there either." He paused. "I saw her leave with my own eyes."

Kanati glared at him. "What you mean leave?"

"You heard me." He wiped his mouth with the back of his hand. "She left. With your friend. That dude you brought with you. The one who bought the sheep and—"

Kanati took one step back, his brother's words too hard to bare or to understand. Besides, he didn't make any sense. Sunni would never leave the reservation without him. She said it herself. "You don't know what you talking about, nigga."

"Your brother is a liar but he's telling the truth this time." Paco's friend added. "I saw them leave too, Kanati. Hand in hand they left this reservation. I promise."

Kanati ran through the house quickly while the world felt like it was spinning under his feet. His research didn't take long to come to an end. Sunni had left. Although her clothing was there it was obvious that she was gone when he noticed the pictures of her mother and father missing.

Walking back outside, he ran a hand down his face and flopped into one of the white plastic chairs by the front door. "Why...why would she do this?" He said mostly to himself. "I don't understand."

"Come on, man," Paco said playfully, walking up to him. "You know that woman always been out your league." He laughed at his own humor despite the cold moment. "I'm surprised you had her this long."

Kanati heard his brother but he was in another world. As he sat in that seat, heavy with emotions of hurt, betrayal and hate, he wondered whom he would kill first to make the pain go away.

It had been a long time since he felt that type of rage. In fact the last time he felt anything similar he had just found out that his African American mother and Native American father, who were both citizens of the United States, died in the war on Afghanistan. Not having any other viable relatives of age, he was forced to live on a reservation with people he never met, including his drunken brother by his father. And still, even that pain he felt after losing his parents didn't compare to what he felt now.

As he sat on that chair, gazing into the horizon it was as if he were changing inside. Once a warm loving person, he was now filled with hate and was on the verge of exploding.

Nothing would be the same.

This was certain.

CHAPTER THREE

LAW

Law sat in the back of his father's strip club in the VIP section as music thundered from the speakers sending everyone into a money-spending-sex-filled frenzy. Although originally for men only, Jimmy's Palace quickly picked up a strong loyal female fan base. Besides, many eligible men were in the building and single women looking to imprint upon dudes already in the laid back mood knew it was the perfect place to get wifed.

The baddest strippers Baltimore had to offer hung totally naked from the ceilings dripping in gold chokers and crystal clear high heel shoes. Everything in that bitch sparkled and glistened. The floor beneath the dancers was littered with so many bills it looked like grass.

Sitting on a burgundy sofa, Law inhaled the sweet smoke from an expensive cigar. Moozy, L.F., Petey and Vanessa sat on the long couch with him as a bartender poured champagne into their glasses like water from a faucet. Every so often the best trap niggas in the city would be allowed to step up and enter the VIP area to give Law dap. Most at the very least respecting his hustle, not to mention he was building a lucrative Percocet and Molly business.

Loving the limelight and adjusting one of the two gold chains on his chest, Law sat deeper into the seat when *Digital Dash* by Drake & Future boomed from the speakers. Within seconds Sunni became visible in the doorway and time appeared to stop. Wearing everything *Versace*, she swung her long flowing hair and placed one hand on her hip as she stared seductively at Law across the room.

It was a wrap.

She had arrived.

The attention was immediately sucked from the strippers and placed on Sunni. The black dress hugged her hips and her breasts were just high enough to kiss.

Why do she have to be so fine? He thought.

When Law winked, she swung her hair again and strutted slowly toward him. Talk about bundles. Her silky black mane blinged so hard the hairdressers in the building wondered where she bought her tresses, not knowing every strand was hers. Every nigga in the building wanted a taste, touch and fuck. Too bad for them she was off limits.

When she made it to Law she slowly sat on his lap and placed a hand on his cheek. Looking into his eyes, she smiled and slobbed him down. When she was done their lips separated and she said, "Thank you for saving me."

Niggas were sick with the flu as they watched them together, realizing she could never be had. So what was left to do but to congratulate the man on scoring such a treasure? One by one hood entrepreneurs shook Law's hand for pulling the beautiful thoroughbred, all wishing they were in his shoes.

Law's chest was so swollen he could've floated away if there was no roof. He knew landing her would increase his rep, which is why he went all the way across America to get her, but the recognition was more than he saw coming.

With all the pride in the world he looked into her eyes and said, "Who gonna stop us now?"

"Nobody," she said kissing him again. "Nobody."

KANATI

Kanati walked into the small billiard bar on the reservation where his friends were playing pool. The moment they saw his face they knew all hell was about to be unleashed. And as close as they were, they were willing to die in the fire with him if it be his will.

Concerned, they tossed down their pool sticks on the table and walked toward him. "She left you didn't she?" Micco asked Kanati as they surrounded him. At 5'11 Micco was relentless. He enjoyed battle so much that there was a running joke that he drank blood for breakfast. And since the rumors were mostly true he never denied the claims.

Upon hearing his statement Kanati moved uneasily where he stood. He had come to tell his friends how he'd been played and it appeared they knew more about Law than he did. But how? "You knew?" Kanati asked him and the others.

They all looked at one another clearing their throats.

"We ain't know he was gonna rob shawty from up under you but we weren't feeling the boy Law at all," Shilah responded, his shoulder length hair tamed with a black bandana. Out of the group it was he who spoke wisdom whenever necessary. And since depression was heavy where they lived his words of prudence were required often.

"That's why we left the party early," Bidzil added. "The way he was eying Sunni ain't feel right, man." Bidzil, a self-proclaimed sex addict, was the only member of the group who didn't have hair. Intentionally bald, he preferred it that way so there would be nothing to maintain.

"But why you didn't say something?" Kanati glared at them.

"Bruh, the way you were acting we figured you wanted him to have her." Micco said scratching his low cut hair. "I even saw you looking at him a few times when he was checking her out."

Law ran his hand down his face trying to play the tapes back in his mind although he was running a blank. He couldn't recall one moment when Law was looking at Sunni the wrong way. "Fuck no I didn't see that shit."

"How were we to know?" Micco continued. "If you didn't see it you were blind. Anyway, Sunni always been a little disrespectful when it came to—" Shilah slapped him in the chest, stopping his sentence.

Everybody knew Sunni was no good but they loved Kanati too much to say a word. Their silence was not because they wanted to keep the truth away from their man but because they told him before that she was off and he grew violent. And still, all of them could recall Sunni telling stories about her dreams for living the luxurious life. And since Kanati was barely making ends meet they knew her leaving would be a matter of time.

Kanati looked down. "I'm not gonna be right after this shit."

They all looked at each other. "All you gotta do is tell us what you need from us." Bidzil said rubbing his hands together. "And it's on."

"Yeah, Kanati," Micco said with a sinister look. "We going to Baltimore or what?"

Kanati was sitting in front of his house when Nanni walked up to him. Her silky long hair blew in the soft wind. Standing in front of him she said, "Don't go, Kanati. Please."

He looked up at her. "You can't ask me something like that, Nanni." He looked away. "You know that."

She sat next to him, eyes now on the horizon. Taking a deep breath she said, "If you go you will bring hell back here like you can't imagine. And I will die in this war too." She paused. "Kanati, I have seen it in my dreams. Many times."

He shook his head. "Nanni, don't say things like that," he said seriously. "First of all it's not true. I'd never let anything happen to you."

"If you go back to Baltimore I will die." She paused. "And you will lose a lot avenging my death. Maybe even your soul."

He exhaled with agitation.

He loved his grandmother but sometimes her hold on him prevented him from living his best life. Had it not been for Nanni he would've done everything illegal he needed to do to give Sunni the life she wanted but he promised Nanni he was done with everything foul.

And now look.

He lost his bitch.

"So I'm supposed to let him come into my home and disrespect?" He said through clenched teeth. "Are you actually saying this to me?"

"Kanati, have you ever wondered why it was so easy for you to bring him here?"

Silence.

"Everyone could see that boy's evil intentions but you," she continued. "It was as if you were temporarily blinded so that you wouldn't interfere with the scheme of it all." She paused. "In other words it was God's plan to get that girl away so He shielded Law's dark energy from you."

He sighed. "I didn't expect this. I would've never brought him here had I known."

"Don't you see what I'm saying, Kanati? That's because you *weren't* supposed to *see*. You were supposed to *allow*. She was supposed to go with him because she was never meant for you." She placed a hand on his heart. "When you are embraced in love, as you are, the universe caters to your every need but first it has to make a way. And Sunni was in the way so she's gone. Let her be." She paused. "Don't get me wrong, she is beautiful but that rots with time. It's all about the heart." She touched his hand and gripped softly. "Let her go, son. And I promise what's in store for you will thrill you in ways you can't imagine." She smiled but then grew serious. "But go against God's will and many will die."

Kanati continued to gaze outward, his nostrils flaring in quick short puffs. His temples throbbed as thoughts of Law making love to Sunni crowded his mind. Normally his grandmother could speak to that part of him that understood what she was saying but now, well now the old woman failed miserably.

Frustrated and in pain, he stood up and walked in front of her. His eyes were glassed over and suddenly he looked like a different man. A man capable of atrocities that would be hard to imagine.

"I suggest you start praying," he said before walking away.

Sunni was smiling as she got out of the taxi in front of Law's father's mansion. Loaded down with Louis Vuitton bags and the like, she was already acclimated to her new life. If Law did anything it was make good on his promise to spoil her more rotten than bad meat. She was in luxury heaven. When they weren't shopping he was showing her off around town or taking her to the best parties. All in all it was the best decision she'd made to leave Arizona.

Sunni was just about to walk into the house after her shopping spree when she saw Kanati step from behind the large tree in the front yard. His hands clasped behind him, his curly hair pushed backwards with a black bandana.

The moment she saw him her jaw dropped. "What…what are you—"

"Come here." He said softly. "I gotta talk to you for a minute. You owe me that much."

"You're gonna hurt me."

"Have I ever laid a finger on you?"

She was about to ask the cab driver for a ride away but he pulled off before she could make the request. Realizing she had to get it over with, she placed the bags on the ground and trudged toward him. "When did you get here?" She whispered. "And are you alone?" She looked behind him for Micco and the rest of his crew.

"Why, baby?" He asked in a low voice. His heart was broken and he tried to maintain face but it was difficult. At the end of the day she destroyed him more than he thought a person who claimed to love him ever could. And all of this without so much as a letter. "Why did you have to do it like that?" He paused. "If you wanted to go, that was your choice but like that? In front of my friends? And family?"

She crossed her arms over her chest tightly. "You know what, I told you what I was gonna do, Kanati. I wanted more." She unfolded her arms and threw her hands up in the air. "And you couldn't provide that for me. So the question is, what are you doing here now?" She paused. "Oh so, what, you trying to ruin my life now and take away my happiness?"

"Never, baby. I would never want anything but your happiness." He looked at her for what seemed like forever. "I'm here because, well, I just wanted to see your face."

"And did you get a good fucking look?" She stuck her neck out and tilted her head.

He frowned, not believing how cold she was acting. It was as if he never met her until this very moment. "Yeah." He nodded. "I got a good look. Finally."

"Good, I mean, what's your purpose anyway? I'm never going back with you."

"All I wanted to know was if I should bring war on this city." He paused. "That's why I'm here."

She stuck her head out like a long necked goose. "Well?" She asked in an uncaring way. "Have you decided? Because to be honest you're getting on my fucking nerves right now."

He stared at her for a little longer. Her eyes were cold and her energy felt off, as if she were possessed by money or something much darker. All had become clear. His grandmother was right after all. She was never his. "Now I know that the snake really did me a favor by taking you away." He exhaled in a sigh of relief and she noticed the anger going away and being replaced with calmness. "I mean, I really dodged a bullet." He ran his hand down his face, as everything around him suddenly seemed brighter. "I had been tripping this entire time."

She was surprised and embarrassed at his response. Knowing the things that Kanati was capable of when he got angry she was sure he would flip over the city to win her back. Had warned her mans and all. But now, well now she felt stupid. "So you expect me to believe you came all this way for nothing?"

He nodded and smiled for the first time in the two weeks since she'd been gone. "Yep." He paused. "Because you were never worth it. Just took me longer to see that's all."

Kanati turned to walk away.

Humiliated that he hadn't started the war that she told Law to expect, she wanted to hurt him. But she also knew putting her hands on him would be futile and could very well mean the end of her life. But what was she to do with all of the anger she felt?

All the man did was walk away and still she was raging up as if he had smacked her or stomped on her toe. Before he showed up she was living the life she thought she wanted and now it felt as if all the unhappiness that he had sat with for weeks had been transferred onto her and she hated him for it.

"Fuck you!" She yelled as he continued to walk up the street without a care in the world. "Fuck you, Kanati Dawson! I hate you and I hope you die!" She yelled, spit flying from her mouth as tears rolled down her cheeks. "Do you hear me? I hope you die!"

Two hours passed since Kanati walked away forever and the only thing that changed was the level of Sunni's anger. On a scale of one to ten her piss-ness was multistory. Feeling unable to walk because her muscles were so tensed all she could do was sit on the sofa and cry. Surrounded by brown Louis Vuitton bags and baby blue Tiffany boxes it was apparent that she was still unhappy. It was then that she realized even when you move into luxury you take your depression and pain with you if you aren't happy or don't know yourself.

Everything felt worthless and stupid.

"I made a mistake," she said to herself, realizing she really did love Kanati at that very moment. While also knowing it was too late. He would never take her wretched ass back. "What have I...what have I done?"

Slowly she got up from the sofa, roughly wiped the tears away and walked toward the back of the mansion. Once in the garage she grabbed a red plastic container of gasoline and a box of matches from the top shelf. Next she opened the three-car garage and walked toward the guesthouse where Kanati once lived.

Opening the door she poured gas all over the house, being careful to douse every inch, especially his bed. When everything was as wet as her tears she strutted back to the front door. Before lighting the match she looked around. Now hysterical crying consumed her and she couldn't bring herself to stop.

Sunni, a full-blooded Navajo Indian, was deeply troubled in more ways than most people knew. Usually folks only saw her beauty. It was Kanati who accepted her as she was, despite her upbringing. Thereby seeing through her interior. Who would love her unconditionally now?

But who gave a fuck at this point?

She was Law's problem.

Striking the match on the side of the box she tossed the lit stick onto the floor and walked out, sending flames throughout the guesthouse in the process.

Law walked toward his car in the back of one of his father's strip clubs only to see Kanati leaning against Law's black BMW, arms crossed over his chest as if it were his. Law reached for his hammer before realizing he left it at home.

"Fuck," he said to himself.

The plan was to take his new girl out on the town and show her off again later, so Law didn't want to be strapped. But now he believed it was a big mistake.

"Got a second?" Kanati asked calmly.

Law nodded realizing it was time to face the music. It wasn't like Sunni didn't warn him that Kanati would soon be returning, he just thought with the passage of time that Kanati knew that he lost her for good. It had been two weeks after all. So why was he here now?

Law strutted up to him. The smile Law was accustomed to seeing on Kanati's face was an after thought. Now he looked like a man who killed many, and Law wondered if Petey was right. Was there something about the soft breaded man that he missed?

"If you coming back for her, you can forget about it, bruh." Law said sinisterly. "She done already took this dick. That means she's ruined for you forever."

Kanati laughed. "Is that right?"

"Yep." Law rubbed his hands together. "She been waiting on a nigga and everything. Said it with her own lips."

Kanati nodded. "Why was it so easy being foul? I opened my home to you and you carried it hard."

Law laughed once. "I don't know, bruh. Why was it so easy being soft?"

"Even still you know nothing about me." Kanati glared. "If you did you would be more careful with what you say."

Law clapped several times. "Trust me, I know all I need to know 'bout you." He paused. "Including how you took me to your hood and let me snatch your bitch from up under you."

"If I wanted to, I could kill you now." Kanati said. "And I want you to remember that I'm making a conscious choice to leave you alive." Kanati stepped closer. "Besides, you 'bout to get everything you deserve and more," Kanati nodded, referring to Sunni. "So get ready." He walked away.

"What does that mean?" Law yelled to his back. "I asked what the fuck does that mean?!"

Law, his father and Sunni stood on the lawn as they watched the fire fighters attempt to save the back of the house. Although the guesthouse was completely destroyed, there was still hope for the mansion although as the fire grew brighter even that looked impossible.

"How did this happen?" Jimmy asked touching the sides of his face as his possessions went up in a blaze. "I've lost everything I owned."

"I don't know, pop," Law said as he watched the flames. "I'm...I'm so sorry." He looked at him and back at his house. "This shit is fucking crazy."

Jimmy placed his hand on his son's shoulder. "We gonna build again." He took a deep breath. "Just gonna take awhile that's all."

Sunni grabbed Law's hand and softly tugged him a few feet away from Jimmy. When they were out of hearing range she said, "I know who did this to your house." She wiped tears away, her long hair now resting in a messy bun on top of her head.

"What...what you talking about?" He frowned.

"It was Kanati."

He pulled out of the hold she had on him and pointed at the house. "Are you saying that nigga did—"

"I know it's horrible but you need to know the truth," she said cutting him off. "He came by earlier and begged me to go with him and I refused, Law. I love it too much here and I loved being with you." She sighed deeply. "So this is how he showed his rage.

And you must make him pay. You must take everything away from him that he took from us."

Law stepped away from her, his heart thumped powerfully in his chest. "But that nigga's a clown."

She took a deep breath and shook her head softly from right to left. "There are some things about Kanati you need to know if you're going to step to him." She looked down and back into his eyes. "Before you met him, him and his friends robbed and killed a lot of people back in the day. But Kanati felt guilty and tried to change his life around." She sighed deeply.

"But I guess losing me was too much for him to bare." She continued, looking at the burning house. "So he did this." She moved closer. "The thing is this...if you step to him you have to kill him, Law. You can't leave him alive. It'll be like having a wild animal loose in your house. If you step to him and don't kill him, he won't stop until he destroys everything you love. But it'll be slow and painful and not quick and fast like you may imagine."

"What you saying?"

"That he will never stop until everything you know is dead. And then he will kill you last. It's in his nature."

Law placed his hand on his forehead and the other on his hip as he looked at the burning house again. He had seen Kanati earlier so he knew she was speaking the truth about him being in town. Still, Kanati being involved in the robbery and murder game was too much to believe. Sounded like fiction to him.

Suddenly he remembered when Kanati said you will get what you deserve. And he figured this was what he meant by his statement. Filled with rage, Law looked at her once and walked away.

"Law!" Sunni yelled walking toward him before stopping in her tracks. "Where are you going?"

Sensing something was off Jimmy turned around to see his son leaving the scene. "Son," he paused. "What's wrong?" Law continued to walk. "We will rebuild don't worry! Son, where are you going?"

CHAPTER FOUR

KANATI

ONE WEEK LATER

Kanati was riding in a van sitting in the back leading toward his reservation in Arizona. He had been missing in action electing to take a brief sabbatical for a week to get his mind off Sunni by being in isolation and it worked. He was finally starting to realize that maybe things did happen for a reason.

Would he meet someone better with time? Or remain single forever? And now after not talking to his family and friends in days, because he tossed away his cell phone to get silence, he was ready to face them.

But the moment the van stopped at the reservation he noticed that the landscape seemed changed. Structures were grey with smoke soot and some homes were burned to the ground.

But why?

Confused, Kanati hopped out not being able to believe his eyes. What was going on with his home? His friends who were removing debris saw him and rushed toward him the moment he stepped out the van. "Man, where have you been?" Micco asked anxiously. "So much shit done kicked off around here! Why you ain't answer your phone?"

"What, what happened?" Kanati asked looking behind him at the destroyed reservation. His house, his grandmother's and many other homes were burned to the ground. He could barely breathe or catch his breath.

"That dude," Bidzil said placing his hands on his head, looking back at the reservation. "He brought some niggas back and they burned most of the houses. Only about seven are left."

"For...for what?" Kanati yelled looking at them. "I don't understand. I mean, he got Sunni. Fuck he want with us?"

"I don't know why either, man." Bidzil said. "And Easy at the hospital with his mother now. They lost everything and she had a nervous breakdown. It's bad."

"There's more, Kanati," Shilah said looking at his friends before his gaze fell on Kanati again. "They got Nanni and...and your brother was murdered too. They shot him in the head when he tried to help her."

Law, Moozy, L.F. and Petey were in L.F.'s basement in east Baltimore, looking at Nanni who was tied up with thick rope to a wooden chair. Even after the four-day drive it took to snatch and bring her from Arizona to Maryland, she still seemed unbothered which irritated Law beyond belief. It was as if she'd come to terms with her death and made peace without his permission.

The fact that she spoke zero English didn't help smooth things over either. He wanted the woman to beg for mercy and at the very least tell him why her grandson burned down his father's home. Which Kanati didn't of course. The flames not only displaced them from the mansion but since the fire department was ruling it arson, they were under investigation, which meant the insurance would not pay the claim.

Walking up to Nanni, Law slapped the old woman and her head rotated quickly to the left. Unscathed, slowly she turned her head until she was facing him again, her teeth now cranberry red, her eyes wild with fire.

In her native language she said, "Hold tight to those you love. For your time with them will soon come to an end."

Law looked at his friends and back at her before breaking out into heavy laughter. "I don't know what you're saying but everything that happened was your grandson's fault. He shouldn't have fucked with me and—"

RING. RING. RING.

Law removed the cell phone from his pocket and showed the screen to his friends. "Must be that nigga." With a smile on his face he pressed the button to answer. "'Bout time you got back at—"

"Where is she?" Kanati asked calmly.

Law smiled. "Right here."

"Give her back to me." He paused. "You do this and the only person I will kill will be you and one more for the trouble. You can pick the other family member."

Thinking him a fool, Law laughed loudly and looked at Moozy, L.F. and Petey. While Moozy and L.F. thought the show was hilarious Petey walked up the steps and out the basement. Besides, Petey knew things would reach this level and now it was too late to stop future chain of events.

Law shrugged when Petey walked away and focused back on the phone. "We both know that ain't happening. What I'm gonna do is kill this bitch tonight. What you got to say 'bout that?"

Kanati took a deep breath. "First I'm gonna hit your city. Then I will kill every nigga you know. Then finally, I will kill you."

Law, although surprised at the calmness in Kanati's voice, still thought the man too soft to be taken seriously. "Come on, bruh." He chuckled. "You ain't no villain. You one of the good guys."

"What are you gonna do?" Kanati asked firmly.

"I'm not giving you —"

CLICK.

"Hello," Law said into the phone. "Hello." He looked at the screen and realized that Kanati had ended the call abruptly. He had to admit, Kanati's voice didn't possess the distress he thought he would receive when he killed his brother, kidnapped his grandmother and burned down half of the reservation. He seemed like it was just another day in the hood and that was somewhat unsettling, although he'd never let his friends know.

Stuffing the phone back into his pocket he took a deep breath and shrugged. "Guess your grandson doesn't care about you after all." He paused. "Didn't even wait for my demands."

She smiled.

"Um, let me see what's wrong with Petey right quick," he told his boys. "Keep an eye on her."

Law took another deep breath and bopped up the steps. He was trying to rid himself of the nagging feeling that suddenly came over him. Did he make a mistake by moving so callously? The sensation that chilled his bones was the unsettling fear of realizing that maybe he had gone too far.

And more than that…maybe it was too late.

When he reached the top he saw Petey sitting at L.F.'s dirty kitchen table smoking a cigarette. "What's wrong with you?" Law asked. "Why you leave like that?"

"I think you fucked up majorly." Petey said with zero fucks to give. "My position hasn't changed."

Law started laughing. "Wait, you scared of Chief?" He questioned as if he wasn't shook a little. "That niggas soft, Pete. Trust me."

"It ain't about being scared or soft. I warned you this would happen, man. I warned you and now look. I personally think he has the skills for the fight ahead of us. But do you?" He took another pull and blew smoke into the air.

"I got guns." He sat back and tapped the table a few times with his index finger. "And niggas to pull the triggers too."

"Nah, you got clowns. And niggas who never busted shit but a nut." Petey shook his head. "Do you know what I was doing when I was looking around your guest house where he stayed the day we were going to that party?" He paused. "When I found the picture of Sunni?"

Law shrugged.

"Researching." Petey continued. "At first it was just because I wanted to know if we should be having him around us. But later I found out he was different and I learned a lot about him." Petey paused. "The books by Robert Greene on his shelf told me he was calculating. The silver bars over every doorway for pulling himself up and the heavy weights in his room indicated he was strong. The knife collection on the wall said he was vicious. And the shrine he had for his grandmother in the living room told me he adored her. I mean did you even look, man?"

Law scratched his head. "Nah, I ain't see all that shit." He waved the air. "I'm strong and vicious too though." He shrugged. "Fuck I care?"

"You don't see because your vision is too narrow and you think everything's a joke." Petey said seriously. "This nigga lifted a car with me and you in it to change a tire." He leaned in. "Meanwhile you got winded when we jogged around the block last week."

Law glared at him. "I did a search on YouTube, Pete." He waved the air. "Plenty of niggas can lift cars." He shrugged. "It ain't no big deal."

"But can you?"

Silence.

Law leaned forward and clutched his hands in front of him tightly on the table. "So what you saying, man? Huh? You backing out on me now? After this dude burned down my father's house?"

"Nah. I ain't going nowhere. I don't leave my friends when a battle starts." He paused. "But I do know this, if you want a chance at survival you better start listening to me. Otherwise none of it will matter because we'll be dead niggas walking." Petey got up and walked away.

CHAPTER FIVE
EAST BALTIMORE

The city was dark and the sounds of sirens, fights and the like hung in the air like an invisible veil. Jake and Newton, two low-level trap niggas, were in the alley getting money. To the right and left of them were red brick walls belonging to apartment buildings and in the back of them was a green dumpster and behind it was another building. Objectively speaking they were blocked in if something vile were to kick off and sadly for them, it was.

Still, it was a perfect place to do dirt, without irritating the older neighbors who had grown ill of the constant drug dealings in their community.

When Newton, who was twenty-five and had Jake by two years in the game, got hunger pangs that started to rock his gut, he looked to his young compeer to soothe the pain.

Scratching through his bushy rows of braids with fingernails the color of soot, he said, "I'm hungry as a bitch, yo." He dug into his pocket. "Go get me a lake trout sandwich and old bay fries with a half and half."

He handed him some money and stuffed the rest back in his pocket.

"But I'm still getting paper out here." Jake said, his eyebrows so thick folks wondered how he saw.

Newton frowned upon hearing his combat. "If you don't take your bushy fucking eyebrows the fuck out of—"

"Aight!" He yelled, hating getting clowned. With the money in tow he made a quick U-Turn for the exit. "I be back."

"Well hurry the fuck up." When he was gone Newton turned around to piss. Releasing his dick from his pants he was humming *No Limit* by *G-Easy* as he allowed the liquid to flow freely from his body. Looking down at the ground, he aimed his urine at the rat that had been hanging in the area all night until suddenly he heard a whistle above him.

Gazing upward he was shocked to see a nigga in blue jeans and no shirt, standing on top of the dumpster, looking down at him. A black bandana was on his head and his long braids extended from it like black octopus tentacles except the tips of each braid were now died silver in honor of his grandmother.

"What the fuck is you?" Newton asked, backing up to the wall, dick still hanging free. "How did you get over here?" He tried to grab his gun but dropped it on the ground.

Kanati hopped off the dumpster, kicked the gun away, rushed up to him and shoved him against the wall. Once there he placed his hand over his dry lips and brought a knife across his throat while silencing his screams.

No explanations given.

Dead, Newton slid to the ground and Kanati lowered himself, carving a V on his forehead.

"Aye, yo, you didn't give me enough money for the—" Jake had walked in on the scene and was shocked at Kanati standing over his friend's bloodied body like a predator. He tried to turn around and run but was unable to when Micco, Bidzil and Shilah walked up behind him pushing him closer to Kanati. Each was wearing a black bandana to express unity.

Jake was horrified. "Aye, man, I don't know what he did but I won't say nothing," he pointed down at him. "Especially if this 'bout the girl he raped. I barely touched her. You can ask anybody. It was all—"

Micco stole him in the face, silencing him instantly. Shilah pushed him closer to Kanati, Jake shivered as he looked down at Newton, wondering if his own fate would be similar. "I'm gonna say something to you that I want you to tell the city."

"Whatever it is I'll tell them." Jake said shook.

"Nobody eats until Law Hightower is six feet deep."

"Okay, okay," Jake said, shaking his head rapidly. "I'll let niggas know."

Suddenly his shirt was lifted up and Bidzil slapped a firm hand over Jake's mouth from behind to conceal his scream. Wondering what was happening, he soon got his answer when Micco brought the blade of the knife across his belly, digging into his flesh, past the fatty tissue but stopping short of going too deep. When he was done, the letter V was present.

When his friends were finished Kanati looked at the weeping man. "Now go. Let the city know that nobody is off limits."

J-Five and Hershey had run to the top level of an abandoned Baltimore City row home tripping and geeking hard. After robbing a few unsuspected trap boys who weren't prepared for the corrupt twosome, they were eager to divide up their money, find another dealer and get high.

J-Five, whose hair was so thick he couldn't get a finger through it let alone a comb, walked into a bedroom with Hershey, a lanky ex-dealer with a gripe against the world following behind, almost tripping over his own feet. Tossing the money and drugs in the corner they were about to divide up the booty when all of a sudden J-Five looked up in horror.

Sliding into the window was Kanati wearing no t-shirt and blue jeans while holding a crusted bloody knife in his hands. The tips of his braids being silver gave him a villainous façade. Stepping closer, Kanati whistled.

Thinking Kanati was with the dudes they robbed moments earlier J-Five immediately copped a plea. "I'm sorry, man." He paused, white palms in Kanati's direction. "Hershey told me to do it but them guns ain't loaded." He tossed one out of his pocket and it clanked against the hard floor. "I wasn't gonna hurt 'em. I promise."

"How you sound?" Hershey pointed at himself after hearing his friend throw him under the train. "I ain't pick them niggas out. You did!"

Kanati slowly walked toward Hershey who pulled out another revolver from the back of his pants. "Don't come near me!" Hershey yelled, gun shaking in his hand as he aimed at Kanati. "I'll shoot! I swear to God I'll shoot."

Kanati smiled and continued to move closer with no fear in his heart available. Once he was within touching distance Kanati laid hands on the man by hitting him in the nose and kicked the gun when it hit the floor, sending it spinning across the room. Afterwards Kanati picked up a loose piece of concrete cylinder and dropped it on his head. He was out.

Seeing his boy take a hard fall J-Five ran toward the exit but was hit so hard in the face by Micco he was knocked asleep.

Now they both were out cold.

Bidzil and Shilah entered the room from the door.

Ten minutes later Hershey was awaken to something warm and wet splashing against his cheeks. His head rocked due to the pain he experienced by the cylinder and the pain was blinding. When he opened his eyes and looked up at Bidzil who had his dick out and was pissing all over his face he wanted to pass out again. "What the fuck?" He yelled wiping his face erratically with his hand as he slid back into the wall. "What's going on?"

Bidzil laughed, tucked his dick and moved to the side as Kanati approached Hershey. Staring down at him Kanati said, "Nobody eats until Law Hightower is six feet deep."

When Hershey looked across the room he saw J-Five propped up against the wall directly across from him. His shirt was off and a letter V was carved into the brown flesh of his belly. Squiggly lines of red blood eased from his pink open tissue and dripped into his lap.

Hershey almost passed out again until Bidzil slapped a hand across his mouth as Micco ripped into the skin of his forehead with the letter V for villains. He tried to scream out at the pain but the press on his mouth was official and he could barely move his lips. "Tonight you have been spared." Kanati said standing in front of him, his men behind him like crazed sidekicks. "Stay off the streets. It's a state of emergency."

Kanati walked out and Bidzil, scratching his baldhead looked back at Hershey once more with a smile as they all piled out, bloody knives in hands.

Kenny and Jordan were in the trap house bagging dope in the quick and mechanical way they had become accustomed. Downstairs were two of their partners protecting the entrance from the outside with their lives to be sure the operation wasn't hindered by thievery. The risk of robbery was heavy in the hood so they had to be prepared for anything.

Except this night they weren't.

"Yo, let me get a fug right quick," Kenny said taking his gloves off and tossing them on the table littered with small bags and drugs.

"Fuck that," Jordan said pointing at him. "I'm tired of you smoking up my shit." Jordan removed his gloves and tossed them on the floor. He walked to the window, opened it and sat on the ledge. A warm breeze rolled inside. "Get yah own." He removed the cigarette box from his pocket, slid one out and stuffed it back in his pocket before dipping in the other one for a red lighter.

"Fuck is you talking about, yo?" Kenny said walking up to him. "As many fugs as I give you?"

Jordan waved his hand, placed the cigarette in his mouth and lit it. The tip glowed orange. Pulling deeply he released smoke into the air. "Nigga, suck my-"

Suddenly there was a loud and panicked scream that jolted Kenny to the core.

At first Kenny thought Jordan had fallen out the window because he was yanked so quickly it was as if he morphed to some strange place within time. His suspicions were all over the place until Kanati walked inside the same window his man disappeared from and stood before him, whistling lightly.

"Who the fuck are you?" Kenny quickly moved for his gun in the next room until he was hit on the back of his head by Kanati, falling face first to the grungy floor. When Kenny rolled over, nursing the knot forming in the back of his head, he was looking up at Kanati, Bidzil, Shilah and Micco. "Fuck is this about, yo? Yah 'bout to get blasted in this bitch. You better leave."

Kanati stooped down, released the knife from the holder he had on his lower leg and smiled. Picking his nail with the tip of the blade he calmly said, "Scream."

While waiting for him to comply, Bidzil and Shilah went downstairs while Micco stayed with Kanati.

"Fuck you mean scream?" He tried to scoot backwards but a Timberland boot pressed upon his chest, courtesy of Micco, which stopped his motions.

"I said scream." When Kanati cut a V into his head as Micco held the man down Kenny screamed at the top of his lungs.

A minute later two men rushed through the front door downstairs. Ready to attack, Bidzil knocked out the first man and relieved the second of his gun as Shilah held a knife to his throat, pushing him up the stairs.

Confused, John looked at Kenny who was lying on the floor dead, with a V on his head and then at Kanati and Micco. "I don't know what this is about but please don't do it. This is Tone's place and—" Micco stole him in the jaw, silencing him immediately.

Calmly as usual, Kanati walked up to him. "Tell the city nobody eats until Law Hightower is six feet deep."

John nodded rapidly, hoping to make it out of the situation alive. "Okay, man," he said. "Anything you say."

"Good." Kanati grinned. "Now I have to leave you a little something to remember us by." He moved closer to him, the knife aiming in the man's direction.

Kanati, Bidzil, Micco and Shilah strutted toward their car, tired due to their ferocious adventures. They had a long night of letting their presence be known in Baltimore and now it was time to go to the motel and rest.

As they walked down the street Kanati thought about his grandmother and how she tried to warn him about the darkness coming their way if he headed to Baltimore. It was the one thought that stagnated him at times and caused him to pause with guilt.

Sensing his friend's pain in the moment, Shilah placed a hand on Kanati's shoulder. "We have no time for grief, friend." He said. "We're here. Let's just get this shit over with and try to save her."

Kanati nodded. He knew he was right and prayed for a better outcome while unleashing hell in his stead.

When they made it to the car Kanati opened the driver's side door and put on a fresh white t-shirt. Bare chest the entire time prior, he was ready to come down to earth for the moment until his next venture.

When he was clothed, Micco took the passenger seat and Shilah and Bidzil climbed in the back. They were about to pull off until Kanati realized the car wouldn't start.

"Fuck," he said hitting the steering wheel. "It's not turning on again."

"Please be playing," Shilah said shaking his head before running his hand down his face. "One of us should've stayed out here and kept the car running. You know once this bitch is off it's done for the night."

"Nah," Kanati said yanking the bandana off his head. "I need everybody on deck in case we outnumbered."

"I'm surprised the car made it this far," Bidzil admitted scratching his baldhead. "We actually drove this bitch from Arizona to Maryland with no problem. Guess we got lucky about that part."

Suddenly Micco's eyes lit up with a sinister glow. Kanati only saw this expression when he was up to no good. "I think I can get us a car." With a fixed stare across Kanati and out of the window, Micco observed a female who was parked in a blue 2009 Volkswagen van. She just pulled up across the street and had a passenger in the back that was giving her some money.

Everybody followed his gaze finally understanding he was on some carjacking shit.

"I might have to kill this bitch but so what," Micco said. "We at war." He moved to murder her on the spot and take her car when Kanati slapped a firm hand on his wrist, pulling lightly.

"No women or kids." Kanati said lowering his gaze. "Ever."

"But we need a ride and—"

"No women or kids!" Kanati repeated louder. "No exceptions." He released him and slowly looked over at the young woman in the van. "I'll be back. Sit tight."

Kanati eased out the car, walked across the street and up to the driver's side. The passenger had left and the moment she was about to pull off she saw Kanati standing at her window and smiled. She had never seen anything as sexy as him in Baltimore and immediately knew he wasn't from her city.

Taking one of the tips of his braids she looked up at him. "Silver." She released it. "I like that."

"I have a few questions," he said softly.

"Shoot." She grinned, wiping her gold wild curly hair from her face.

"Do you drive for a living?"

"Yep." She said, nodding rapidly.

VILLAINS: IT'S SAVAGE SEASON   93

"Okay, do you know Baltimore good?"

"Better than most," she shrugged. "I lived here all my life."

Kanati nodded. "Do you have any kids?" That question may have seemed odd but there was a method to his madness. What he was about to ask of the young lady would not be suitable for a mother.

"No, no kids," she smiled. "Now let me ask you a question."

He grinned and placed a hand on the top of her roof. "Shoot."

"Why you asking me so many fucking questions?" She asked jokingly.

He laughed once and covered his mouth with a fist. Her personality was adorable. "I wanna hire you for the next few weeks." He paused. "That is, if you're up for it."

"Yes, of course I am."

"I pay good but that means driving me and my friends everyday, no days off until we finish."

"Finish what?" She asked.

Kanati smiled ignoring her question. "Are you available or not?"

She looked at her watch and said, "Lemme see, it looks like…" she placed her arm down. "I'm available anytime you need me. Even tonight."

He laughed and covered his smile again. "Cool." Although he had been paid nicely from Jimmy before the war began, all of his money went towards the rebuilding of the reservation. So he removed some bills he yanked from the dealers he hit that night from his pocket to pay her. "Let's get to work." He handed her two hundred dollars.

KANATI

Kanati, Bidzil, Micco and Shilah sat in their motel room, smoking weed. When two thick women with fat asses walked by the open window, Bidzil placed his weed out on the wooden bed table and walked toward the door. "I'ma get up with yah later." He gripped his dick.

When his friends saw where Bidzil's gaze fell they shook their heads. "Leave them bitches alone," Micco said scratching his head. "Before they get yah ass in trouble."

Bidzil looked at him, shook his head and bounced out anyway, closing the door behind him.

"So what we gonna do now?" Micco asked as he grabbed his knife and sharpening tool. "I'm ready for—"

"You know this is business right?" Shilah asked, pushing his shoulder length hair back with a bandana, tying it tightly. "We not here to satisfy your blood lust."

Micco chuckled. "Whatever." He sharpened his blade. "If I can kill a few niggas and satisfy the craving at the same time what's the harm in that?"

Kanati ran his hand down his face and chuckled once. "Well I say we hit fifteen more and then we—"

"But we already hit ten," Shilah said.

Kanati shrugged. "And? Why you acting like you ain't know my plans before you got here?" He paused. "City first. Friends second and then Law."

"What about grams?" Shilah continued. "Should we be asking questions to bring her home first? Maybe he ready to let her go now."

"We did that last night after we hit the first five and again he said he not giving her up." He paused.

"But if Baltimore turns on him, a place he loves, he would have to see things our way. Trust me."

"I think we moving further from the goal," Shilah continued. "I mean we thought Micco was after blood but now I'm wondering if it's not you."

Kanati sat back and glared at him. To say Shilah was blowing him was an understatement. Often Shilah carried on like he was somebody's grandfather even though they were all in their twenties.

Frustrated, Kanati took a deep breath and shook his head. Besides, he didn't want to think too much about his grandmother but his heart told him Nanni would be dead in a matter of days if not already.

She predicted it herself.

When there was a knock at the door everybody grabbed their knives and stood on their feet. Kanati moved to the door, pushed the curtain aside and looked out the window. When he got a good view he saw Tammi was on the other side grinning. When he opened the door she saw his friends serious stares and weapons "Wow." She looked at the knives in their hands. "That mad to see me?"

"It ain't like that," Kanati said looking at them and back at her. "I think they need some pussy or something to lighten their mood." He was really referring to Shilah.

She giggled. "I can't help them with that but—" she raised her shirt and flashed her tits before Kanati, embarrassed as fuck, shoved her out the door and closed it behind them.

"What's wrong with you?" He whispered. "Why would you do some shit like that?"

Tammi, who loved a good joke whenever possible, laughed hysterically, until she saw the extreme irritation on his face. "What...it was nothing?" She threw her hands up. "I was just playing since you said they were in a bad mood."

"Well ladies don't play like that."

"And how is that?"

"Like a whore."

The wind blew and she pushed her wild curly hair out of her face. "Well just to be clear, you the one who said something about pussy not me." Embarrassed she crossed her arms over her chest. "Look, I'm sorry." She shrugged. "I'll be more professional in the future." She cleared her throat. "Yah ready to go?"

He looked over her head to the left and then the right. "Yeah, just waiting on Bid to get back. But go warm up the van. We'll be there in a minute."

As she walked away with her head hung low he suddenly felt bad for hurting her feelings. The last thing he needed was to care about another woman while he harbored such a vicious plan for revenge. He wouldn't tell a soul but in the short few days that he'd known her he was pulled to her like a magnet. But what was it? Sure her wide eyes, crazy gold curly hair and pretty smile were appealing but there was something else under the surface he adored.

Even in her crassness, she was the most genuine person he knew.

When he saw her get into the van, he turned to open the door when suddenly he heard Bidzil yell up the block. "Let's get out of here!" He was running toward the van at an extreme speed. "NOW!"

Hearing Bidzil's frantic voice, Micco and Shilah rushed out the room only to see Bidzil dodging toward Tammi's vehicle. Kanati, Shilah and Micco could now see he was in fear for his life and took the hint to heart, all of them running to the van also.

Once inside, Kanati looked at Tammi and yelled, "GO!"

The moment the last door closed and everyone was inside, Tammi pressed on the gas as hard as possible.

The tires left black marks on the ground and smoke in the air.

When she saw two men with hoodies pointing guns at her van she made a quick left in the opposite direction, missing a white Ford Pickup truck by inches. Since the gunmen were on foot and they were driving, bullets flew their way but thanks to her skills, not a one landed.

When they were out of danger Tammi yelled, "What was that about?" She looked at Kanati in the passenger seat and then the rest in the back through the rearview mirror. She was hysterical as sweat poured down her face. "Why were they trying to kill us?"

Kanati, Micco and Shilah all looked at Bidzil, who looked away, out the window, in shame.

"It was nothing, "Kanati said with his eyes still on him. "Sorry about that." He turned to face her and placed a hand on her knee to calm her down. "Just keep driving."

CHAPTER SIX

LAW

Law and Sunni were in the movie theater watching a thriller film while eating popcorn. Every so often he would look over at her and shake his head in awe. She was already a bad bitch but now that he had her icy and dressed to perfection she was all money.

"What you looking at me like that for?" She smiled after catching his gaze.

"No reason." He winked.

She tossed a few kernels of popcorn into her mouth just as the actress in the movie was just about to go into a door where a killer would undoubtedly be waiting. And then..."Aye, Law!" Someone yelled walking inside. "You in here?"

"Shut the fuck up!" A movie patron yelled at him. "Can't you see we watching a film? Damn!"

"Man, suck my dick!" Moozy continued as he walked up the aisle. "Aye, Law where are you? It's Moo! I gotta holla at you about—"

Embarrassed, Law came rushing down the stairs and toward him. Grabbing him by his shirt he quickly ushered him out the theater. It wasn't until they were in the bright area that Law saw Sunni behind him too.

"Man, what you doing?" Law whispered with a glare on his face. "You lost your fucking mind or something?"

"It's worst than me losing my mind, man," Moozy said. "I been hitting your phone for hours. Why you ain't answering?"

"Because I was with my girl," he said pushing his chest once. "Now what the fuck you want?"

"Yeah, Moozy, what's this all about?" Sunni added, whipping her long hair over her shoulder and crossing her arms. As if anyone needed her chimes. "You were very embarrassing back there."

He sighed. "I ain't mean to carry it like that but I think your boy has started already." Moozy said. "A few niggas I know got real fucked up over the past few days and there was one thing they all had in common."

"And what's that?"

"They been saying your name."

"Saying my name?" Law stepped back, looked at Sunni and back at Moozy. "You think this about Kanati?"

Silence.

Law cleared his throat. "But how you know for a fact?" He paused. "You were telling us about a situation last night that sounded on the half."

"Yeah, my bad 'bout that one," Moozy said. "At first I thought the V somebody been carving into dudes stood for Vermont. But now I think it's something else."

"Get to the point," Law said.

"The V is for villains. What you called Kanati on the phone that night." Moozy moved closer to him. "And they were all told one thing. *Nobody eats until Law Hightower is six feet deep.*" He paused. "The nigga been fucking with people money and dude's afraid to trap because they don't know where this nigga's coming from. They also saying he whistles before he kills and I think a few dealers looking to put a bounty on your head behind him. What we gonna do?"

CHAPTER SEVEN

LAW

Sunni was on top of Law, in their twin-sized bed at his much smaller rental home in Randallstown MD. Things were definitely different from the first time Sunni moved from Arizona that was for sure.

With the mansion successfully burned to the ground, Law was waiting on word from his father so that he could move to a new home Jimmy was having renovated. The irony was that Sunni was able to have the luxury life she thought she wanted by leaving with Law but in jealousy mode burned her dreams to the ground with the callous act.

Feeling her body heat up as they made love, Law placed his hands on both sides of her waist and pumped into her while looking up at her beautiful face. Her silky black hair draped her cheeks and brushed his chest as she bit down on her bottom lip. With palms planted firmly on his chest she raised up once and then twice before screaming in ecstasy.

"You feel so fucking good, Sunni," he said as he continued to progress further into her warmth.

"You do too." She lowered her body and kissed him gently as he pumped into her more intensely, her breast mashing against his chest. "Thank you for saving me," she whispered. "I'm falling in love with you, Law Hightower."

"Let me taste that pussy right quick," he said softly. He didn't want to get too romantic that morning because at the moment he wanted to fuck, straight up.

She grinned, rose up and placed her pussy on his lips. Laying her body on his in the opposite direction, she placed his dick into her mouth and suckled while bucking her hips on his face. The sweetness of her pussy and the sensation of her tongue rolling over his shaft and balls had him shivering.

"Fuck," he said as he ran his tongue over her clit and snaked into her dark tunnel. "Suck that dick, bae. Suck that shit real good."

With his wish as her command, Sunni lowered and raised her head repeatedly until she could feel the long vein pulsating on his dick. When it throbbed like soft beats on a drum indicating he was about to explode, she rose up, jumped on his dick and squeezed her inner walls over his thickness. The sensation was so powerful that Law tensed the muscles in his legs and raised his feet slightly off the bed as he splashed into her pussy.

"Fuckkkkkkk!" He yelled experiencing the best orgasm he had in a minute. "Fuck, fuck, fuck!"

She giggled and kissed him again. "So I take it you like that?"

"You wild, bae," he responded slapping her ass once. "That shit was great."

Feeling proud, she fell into him, the top of her head just below his chin. "That was so nice, Law. I feel like you really wanted me." She raised her head and looked up at him. "I mean it was so, so good. And I hope I'm still doing everything to your liking."

He slapped her ass again and she rose up lying beside him on the bed. "Like I said you did shit better than good. As a matter of fact you set my morning right." He slid out of bed and grabbed his navy blue robe sitting on the chair. "But I want you to stop analyzing every time we fuck. It's not that deep."

"I understand, Law and you're right." She wiped her long hair away from her face. "But …uh…I wanted to ask you a question." She sat up, gripped the sheets and covered her body. "Um, I was wondering if I could have some money for—"

"Nah!" He frowned. "I told you times are tough right now, Sunni. And we have to save every dollar we got." He slipped into his robe and grabbed a pack of Black & Mild's off the dresser. "And why you keep asking me for cash when you know shit tight anyway?"

The anticipatory grin she held about getting paid slowly wiped away as she glared at him. "This wasn't the plan when you took me from Arizona, Law." She pointed to the bed. "There were rules and you agreed to obey them."

"That was before your man burned down the house, killing the horses and all other kinds of shit. Don't you get it? Everything messed up now." He removed a Black & Mild, lit it and exhaled, looking up at the ceiling. "I mean can you actually be this fucking greedy? I'm just saying."

"Greedy?" She yelled. "Why do you have to disrespect me like that?"

"It's either greed or selfishness, either way you not understanding my plight right now." He paused. "When Kanati burned down our crib my father had to pour a bunch of money into a new place, which means all of my free cash had to be spent on this crib."

"You mean this dump?" She asked, crossing her arms over her small breasts, the sheet now lying in her lap. "Because as ugly as this house is it should be free."

"This from a bitch who lived in a house made of dirt."

"Fuck you!"

He took another deep inhale and looked at her before exhaling. She was grossing him out with her attitude. Ever since they'd been together he had been given glimpses of her selfishness but now it was growing to disgusting proportions.

She asked for money constantly and he even caught her stealing bills from him one night when he was in bed and she thought he was asleep. And then there were the tiny acts of selfishness when they would go out to dinner and he would ask for a bite of her meal, only to be told no. With a little time he was definitely surprised to see her egotistic side.

When there was a knock at the door he took a deep breath. "Like I said I'm not about to argue with you. The answer is no so don't ask again." To be rude as fuck, he put the cigarette out on one of her Louis Vuitton purses on the dresser and walked out of the room and into the living room.

"Fuck you!" She screamed out.

When he opened the front door Petey, Moozy and L.F. piled inside. Taking a seat on the sofa Law could tell by the way they moved that something was wrong. Needing to see their expressions clearly in the dark space, he turned on the lamp and then pushed back the curtains leading to the balcony across from where they sat. This allowed the sun to enter giving him a better view.

"What's wrong now?" He crossed his arms over his chest.

"It's getting worse," Moozy said removing a Snickers bar from his pocket to take a large bite. "He killed more niggas yesterday. I mean, this dude more annoying than the police. Folks ain't able to move the way they accustomed thinking he gonna get 'em. And everybody blames you. They even calling him the boogie man and shit." He laughed with a mouth full of candy. "I'm talking about grown ass men."

L.F. scratched his burned face and said, "Like he said the worst of it is the streets still mixing your name in the mess. Saying if it wasn't for you this wouldn't be their problem. The whistling shit is creeping them out too. The other day a nigga got banked outside his momma's house just for whistling. His funeral next week. Shit getting crazy." He paused. "I don't know what you have to do but you have to do something, Law."

Law ran his hand down his face and exhaled. "I can't believe this is happening. Like is this dude for real? Somebody gonna put something hot in his head."

Petey smirked, as he continued to play Chess on his phone.

Seeing this snide remark Law walked over to him. "Fuck is that supposed to mean?"

Petey shrugged. "I could say I told you so but it won't do us much good." He sighed deeply. "So for now it's obvious that this situation speaks for itself. And that I warned you."

"Yeah that ain't helping me," Law said walking to the refrigerator and grabbing a beer. Returning back to them he drank half of the can as they watched. "What I need from you is a plan of action."

"Ain't it too early for all that?" Moozy asked, balling up the candy wrapper and stuffing it into his pocket. "The beer?"

"Says the nigga who eating candy at 7:00 in the—" Law's sentence was cut short when Sunni walked out of the bedroom naked. Confused and embarrassed, he rushed up to her and yelled, "Fuck are you doing? Go put some clothes on!"

Law's friends tried not to look but her body was everything so each stole a peek or two for future spank bank reference. And when Law tried to block her frame from their view she slapped him several times in the face until he got out of her way.

With wild crazy eyes focusing on the balcony door, she ran at full speed into it as if she were a delirious deer. The moment her weight met the glass it shattered under her blow and slightly fractured her scalp. She sprung back and landed face up on the floor, blood pouring out of the flesh on her forehead and down into her eyes.

"Call 911!" Law yelled to his friends as he dropped to his knees next to her. "NOW!"

Petey made the call while Moozy and L.F. walked up to him, wondering what they could do to help. A lot became evident to Law as he held the prize he caused a war for in his arms. His precious Sunni was not only selfish but she was also insane.

And still the question was 'What now?'

CHAPTER EIGHT

KANATI

Kanati, Bidzil, Micco and Shilah were sitting in a restaurant preparing to order food. They just finished causing havoc on the city and were famished. When Bidzil saw two sexy women, one with braids and the other with blue faux locs at the table across from them he grinned.

"I'm hungry again but it ain't for food," he said to his friend. "Let me get my relief."

"How 'bout you sit this one out," Shilah said placing a firm hand on his arm.

Bidzil snatched away from him. "I be back, nigga." He looked at Shilah and Kanati. "Order me whatever's hot on the menu." Bidzil slid from the table and introduced himself quickly to the ladies before sitting down without an invite.

"I'm going to get some air." Micco said. "Order me whatever too." He walked away.

Shaking his head, Shilah leaned back and looked at Kanati. He head been wanting to talk to him in private and now his moment arrived. "What's the plan now?"

Kanati thumbed through the menu. "What you talking about?" He frowned and looked up at him before focusing back on the options. "I told you already. First the city. Then niggas he know. Then him."

"Are you gonna call him about Grams again?" He paused. "To check his pressure before we get closer. He gotta have a bounty on him now." He paused. "It's probably the best time."

Kanati slammed the menu shut and ran his hand down his face in frustration. Instead of speaking he remained silent.

"What is wrong with you, man?" Shilah continued. "You going back to the old days when you used to —"

"What's wrong with me?" Kanati yelled. "This nigga disrespected and now I want to get my revenge when —"

Shilah slammed on the table with his fist and then pointed at him. "That's what I'm talking about."

Kanati frowned.

"I thought the plan was to cause problems and force him to release her. Not get revenge alone." Shilah continued. "Has that changed?"

"We doing that, Shilah."

"How?" He shrugged. "By fucking with niggas he don't even know?"

"Nah, by fucking with the city he loves like he did ours," Kanati corrected him. "You don't know this dude, Shi. He lives for people looking up to him. And he won't be able to survive if niggas don't fuck with him no more. So I'm cutting him off at the legs."

Shilah sighed. "Why don't you want to see if she's alive again, Kanati? There has to be a reason."

"Because."

"Because what?" Shilah continued.

"Because I know she's fucking dead already!" He yelled slamming his fist on the table and sitting back in his seat. "And it's fucking me up!"

Bidzil heard the conversation and was about to come back to the table with them until Shilah extended his hand his way, asking him to stay where he was with the women. Bidzil nodded and sat back down.

"She could still be alive, Kanati." Shilah said softly. "Let's find and get her. But if we stay we gonna lose more than we have already."

"Then go back," Kanati said. "I didn't ask you to come."

"But you my friend and—"

"Then ride with me!" Kanati yelled cutting him off. "If you my friend then let me do what I gotta for my peace of mind. If you can't handle it then get on the next plane. Because I'm not leaving until everything Law knows crumbles. That's on —"

"Who is this?" A large man with a smaller man by his side asked stepping up to the table where Bidzil was sitting. Seeing this Kanati and Shilah stood up and approached the group. Bidzil also rose to his feet, preparing for battle.

"You know this dude?" Bidzil asked the female with the locs he was trying to get to know.

"I asked who the fuck are you?" The Angry Man interrupted. "The only one asking questions around here is me."

"Let's roll, Bid," Kanati said to Bidzil. He wanted to keep as low a profile as possible and didn't need the attention. "We can get something to eat later."

The Angry man turned and looked at Kanati with a glare on his face. "He ain't going nowhere until —"

And then shit got crazier.

Nobody saw Micco until he was upon them but The Angry man felt his presence when Micco jabbed him multiple times in the side with his knife bringing him to his knees. It was like a scene from a prison yard movie as blood spurted everywhere and on everybody.

With things out of hand Kanati stole the other man in the face and this set off a major melee that didn't stop until the sirens blasted in the background.

"What's going on now?" Tammi asked returning to the table, placing her phone into her pocket. Blood was everywhere and she was confused. In her opinion she was only gone five minutes and things shouldn't have gotten to that level so soon.

"Let's go! NOW!" Kanati yelled as all of his friends bolted out the door.

CHAPTER NINE

KANATI

Still startled by the scene at the restaurant, Tammi drove silently down the street with Kanati in the passenger seat and Micco, Bidzil and Shilah in the back. Micco and Bidzil were talking loudly about the fight and both were excited about the bloodied outcome. Before leaving the restaurant both perpetrators were on the floor, squirming in their own blood and fighting to stay alive.

Their boasting did nothing but irritate Kanati to no end. The last thing he wanted was his friends causing drama outside of their plans for Law. "Pull over," Kanati said softly to Tammi. "Anywhere."

Tammi looked at him and back at the road. "But we almost off the highway and —"

"I said pull the fuck over!" He yelled louder, silencing Micco and Bidzil instantly.

As she obeyed his command, the tires rolled over granite rocks and sounded like crushed sand until the vehicle stopped on the shoulder of the highway. Annoyed, Kanati pushed the van door open and Bidzil,

Shilah and Micco all crawled out. Cars whizzed by wondering what was going on with the quartet.

The moment Bidzil walked up to Kanati, Kanati hit him in the face, knocking him to his knees.

He leapt back up quickly. "Fuck wrong with you?" He yelled holding his jaw. "You crazy or something?!"

"I'm sick of your shit!" Kanati yelled pointing at him. "That's the second time we had beef because of you."

"Hold up," Bidzil placed a hand over his heart. "That shoot out at the motel wasn't my fault." He looked at Kanati and then Shilah and Micco who looked away, knowing full well he was to blame twice. "I know you not blaming me for that."

"How it's not your fault?" Kanati asked. "You were fucking a bitch and her dude came back to the room." Kanati paused. "This is what the fuck I'm talking about!" Kanati took a deep breath. "I'm here for one purpose and one purpose only," Kanati glared. "To get back at the nigga who killed our people. Not to be fighting over two bitches in a diner you don't even know."

Kanati's words hit Bid to the core. Bidzil, feeling a little guilty that he was a sex fiend, placed a hand on top of his head and the other on his waist. He was about to apologize when he looked into the van and saw Tammi staring at them. "So it's okay for you to carry that bitch around but—"

"Be careful, Bid," Kanati said moving closer. He wasn't keen on women being treated foully, especially those who looked out for him and his crew. "That's my final warning."

Bidzil glared at Tammi again who looked toward the left, at the passing cars on the highway. "You know what, fuck you." Bidzil pointed in Kanati's face and stormed off with Micco following.

Shilah took a deep breath. "I'll go talk to him. It'll be okay." He walked away.

Kanati was sitting in a chair in front of his new motel room smoking a cigarette when Tammi pulled up in her van. She parked, got out and walked toward him. "Are you okay?" She asked softly. "I mean, can I do anything for you?"

He took a deep breath, dropped the cigarette and looked away from her, his hands clutched in front of him.

"Your friends are gonna be fine, Kanati." She said looking at the street and then back at him. "I went looking for them though and couldn't find them anywhere."

He ran his hand down his jeans, stood up and walked toward the entrance. Opening it he walked inside preparing to close it when she placed a flat palm on the door, stopping him from closing it in her face.

Kanati shook his head, trudged away and flopped down on the edge of the double bed with Tammi walking behind him, locking the door. Standing in front of him she removed the black elastic rubber band from her wrist and tied her hair up in a fluffy curly ponytail that sat playfully on top of her head.

"Well, they already think we fucking," she said seductively. "Soooooo, I was thinking we might as well prove them right."

She pushed her jeans down and kicked them off next to the bed. Kanati may have remained silent but looking at her red panties caused him to stiffen. Besides, there was nothing like sex to relieve a little stress.

By T. STYLES

When her jeans were off she removed her shirt slowly. Smiling down at him she pushed down her red panties followed by her red lace bra.

"So you not gonna help me at all?" She said to herself. "Just want me to do all the work while you reap the benefits?" She shrugged. "Okay, I'll play along."

Completely naked she lowered her body and pulled down his zipper; snatching at his jeans and boxers. Before long they lay beside each other on the bed. She grinned when she saw how hard he was. However the grin quickly vanished when she realized how large he was. She didn't know what she expected but it definitely wasn't for him to be packing that much meat.

Bravely crawling on top of him like a climber on Mount Everest, she grinned. "You can fake mad all you want," she smiled. "I know you want this pussy."

"What I tell you about your mouth?"

"Well do something about it."

The moment her warmth covered his dick like a glove her head fell backwards, exposing her neck as she moaned. It seemed like he was pushing inside of her forever but she was trying to be a G and take that D.

Realizing he was probably bigger than the average man, something he'd heard before, Kanati placed his hands on the sides of her waist and pumped into her carefully. There was a mixture of pleasure and pain as Kanati guided her thrusts. And her body trembled as she looked down at him.

"I don't know what's going on, Kanati," she said softly. "But for some reason I feel the need to be here for you. To take care of you. Will you let me?"

"No matter how dangerous shit gets?"

"No matter how dangerous," she said as she lowered her head and kissed him passionately.

CHAPTER TEN

KANATI

Kanati woke up the next morning and looked toward the double bed in the room, which was empty. His friends still hadn't returned and he sighed, hoping they were safe. Shit was turning out to be too heavy in Baltimore but he couldn't go back home until he fulfilled his prophesy for Law's life.

Death to him and all he knew, including Sunni.

When he realized Tammi wasn't in the bed he figured she must have left. For a second their time together flashed back in his mind as he smiled thinking about their sexual episodes. Although falling in love was out of the question because he would never trust another woman, he couldn't deny he was starting to feel her.

Slipping into his boxers he was about to enter the bathroom until he heard whispering inside. Placing his head against the door he heard Tammi speaking lovingly on the phone to someone.

But to who?

Ten minutes later he was sitting outside his motel room smoking when Tammi walked out with a comb and brush. After making love last night they showered and she washed the blood out of his hair. As a result it was wild and curly and since their curl patterns where similar they almost looked related.

With a grin on her face she walked behind him, bent down and kissed his left cheek. "You mad at me?" She asked. "Because I thought I fucked that frown away last night. Why is it back?"

"What I tell you about your language?"

She giggled. "Then what's wrong, Kanati? Seriously."

He shrugged. "Why something gotta be wrong?" He looked up at her. "You got something to hide?"

She cleared her throat. "What? No…of course not." She paused. "I was just asking because you look sad that's all."

He nodded, inhaled smoke before pushing it into the air.

Tammi placed her fingertips in his scalp and massaged lightly before she braided his hair to open his pores. As suspicious as he was about the secret convo in the bathroom in that moment he fell under her touch. No matter what was happening in the world, there was something about a woman that could soothe the savage beast. When he closed his eyes she smiled.

He opened his lids. "Fuck so funny?"

"Nothing." She shrugged. "Just gotta tame this shit that's all. And it has the nerve to be thicker and curlier than mine."

"Do your best," he winked.

She smiled and combed his long hair. "I'm falling for you, Kanati. And as mean as you are—"

"Don't fall for me."

She stopped moving her fingers. "Why not?"

"I'm here for reasons that won't keep me around long." He paused. "And you need to be with a nigga who can treat you how you deserve."

She parted a section of his hair and began to braid tightly and quickly, mad as fuck. "You didn't seem to be rushing back when you were up in this pussy last night. Now all of a sudden Arizona is all the rage?"

He chuckled at her anger just as Shilah and the guys pulled up in a taxi. It was perfect timing too because he wasn't about to argue with her either which way. "Give me some time alone with them."

Mad as a pitbull, she dropped the comb on the ground and stormed into the room.

When the cab parked they all got out and Bidzil stood in front of Kanati, handing him a brown paper bag. "Egg sandwich with cheese. The way you like it."

Kanati accepted the food and that quickly all was forgiven. "Thanks, man." Kanati gave him dap. "I'm hungry as fuck too."

"We been researching our next hit," Shilah said. "Some of Law's friends. I think it's time to advance on your plans."

"Meaning?"

"Hitting the niggas he knows." Bidzil said. "Like the dude Moozy. I'm not sure but I think I may know where his folks live. I asked around and got some answers."

"I'm good with that but only after making a few more moves in the city." Kanati said. "Plus we almost out of money and we'll need funding for our next hits."

Bidzil looked at Shilah and Micco and then walked into the room with Micco. Shilah took a deep breath when they were inside. "I ain't wanna say it but they wanna go home."

Kanati crossed his arms over his chest and sat back in his chair. He figured Shilah had everything to do with the new attitude. "That's different." He paused. "Because Micco loves war and we just getting started."

"His mom died."

Kanati's eyes widened and his arms fell at his sides. "Fuck." He paused, wiping his hand down his face and standing up. "How?"

"Car accident. She was drunk. As usual."

Kanati walked a few feet away. "Definitely go back, man. All of you. I'll take care of whatever I have to here."

"He doesn't want to leave without you, K. Said he can't lose another family member. I just wanted us to make whatever we doing happen quicker. That's the only reason I'm hitting you with this." Shilah paused. "Besides, if we don't move on him now I have a bad feeling. I don't know why."

Across the parking lot Paris was getting into his car. He stopped short when he saw Kanati talking to Shilah outside the motel room. After hearing the legend of Kanati and remembering the description of the nigga terrorizing the city with the silver tipped hair, he was certain he was looking at the same man.

Excited, he removed his cell and snapped a pic of him without Kanati knowing. Next he dialed a number and got into his car, a run down navy blue Impala.

"Hey, where's Tone?" He asked while looking at Kanati and Shilah talking. He was so happy about his find his dick was stiffening.

"He outside." Geez burped. "Why?"

"I think I found that pretty nigga the city been talking about. I'ma text him the pic in a sec." He paused. "Like I really can't believe this shit. The dude is right in front of me, yo."

"You lying, nigga!" Geez said excitedly. "Where you at?"

"Nah. Tell Tone I want my money first. Then we can talk about locations later." He continued. "But trust me. It's definitely him!"

CHAPTER ELEVEN

KANATI

It was nighttime and surprisingly the street was quiet, which was why they chose that particular block. Kanati sat on the top of a brick row house that hosted a liquor store, which was closed for renovations. Above it was two apartments. One on the second floor and the other on the third, both abandoned.

As Kanati looked down, feet swinging off the edge, he was amazed at how many city people didn't look up. They kept their sight eye level so they never saw him until it was too late.

But he saw them.

When he spotted a man and woman walking down the street he zeroed in on them. The man was slapping the woman upside the back of the head as she cried softly, begging him to stop.

Kanati grew angry and whistled to alert his boys he had someone in his sights. Shilah, Micco and Bidzil who were slightly hidden from view heard the call but were confused when Kanati pointed at the couple. The plan was always to go after men in groups of two so that one could pass on the message so what changed?

"Him," Kanati mouthed pointing down at the couple.

Micco who was looking for relief after losing his mother shrugged, stepped out the darkness and hit the man in this face instantly. When the man was on the ground and the woman was stunned and not moving Micco turned to look at her and yelled, "Get the fuck out of here!" He paused. "Now!"

Afraid for her life she took off running and Kanati climbed down the side of the building. However this night wouldn't go as planned like the others. Seconds later three men who knew Barry and saw him get hit came rushing out of a building that Kanati and his crew thought was empty. They had reason to believe this. The windows were broken and the doorway was boarded up. Things had reached a new level for Kanati and his boys because no way were the strangers gonna let Barry get banked.

It was time to engage.

Bidzil hit the first man that stepped up and knocked him against a car with broken windows, which had been there for weeks. With blow after blow he struck him until he was delirious and on the ground. Once back on his feet, Bidzil stomped him until he stopped moving and dragged him into the alley, away from the street.

He wasn't the only one fighting though. Shilah repeatedly hit his opponent in the belly before slamming him on the ground and squashing him in the face with his boot. When the opponent was out cold, and barely alive, Shilah drug him in the alley too.

Kanati also fought his adversary unmercifully. Repeated uppercuts to the jaw and face rendered the man stupid and wobbly as he attempted to fight for his life. After serious many blows, when Kanati saw his opponent's movements were minimal, he stole him one more time, knocking him unconscious.

Glancing over at Micco who was five seconds from killing his man Kanati said to Shilah and Bidzil, "Grab dude!" Kanati pulled his own man toward the alley.

Bidzil and Shilah pulled Micco off the man and it was obvious by the look in Micco's eyes that he snapped a long time ago. Everyone knew that he was still hurting over his mother's death and allowed him the honor to release his frustration.

From where he stood, Kanati looked up and down the street to be sure no one else was coming. They weren't. Dragging his man toward the side door they scouted earlier in the night he dropped his opponent temporarily and opened the door wide. Bidzil dragged Kanati's opponent inside while Shilah yanked Barry, who was Micco's opponent inside the dark room.

Once within the empty dank space that acted as a storage area for niggas who knew about it, the crew forced the men to the ground, their backs against the cool wall. Both spit blood as they looked up at the Arizona natives.

Bidzil closed the door and using the glow from Shilah's iPhone, Kanati walked up to his opponent. "You may not feel like it right now but today is your lucky day."

The man spit blood out and said, "Fuck yah want with me, yo? Huh?" He looked at them and dumped into his pockets, pulling out lint. "I don't got nothing."

"Then you should've minded your fucking business," Bidzil said.

Kanati smiled and walked over to Barry who had been slapping the woman in the back of her head. When he nodded, Shilah and Bidzil removed the man's shirt. "Just out of curiosity..." Kanati said, "Why were you hitting your girl?" He paused. "I just wanna know."

Barry smiled. "Nigga, I know who you are." He grinned wider, his teeth as red as raw beef. "And you got a bounty on your head too. Rest easy tonight, bruh. You won't be alive long." He spit blood again and laughed. "So do what you gotta or suck my—"

The grin was removed when Kanati rammed his knife into the man's stomach. When he screamed out in pain, he slashed the knife across his neck, stood up and looked at his friends.

Slowly they walked over to the last man in the room. "Nobody eats until Law Hightower is six feet deep." He looked at Micco and handed him the knife. "Do the honors."

CHAPTER TWELVE

LAW

Law was walking down the street talking on the phone when suddenly he was hit in the face and caught off guard. The phone dropped out of his hand and spun on the ground before the man stepped on it, crushing the screen. Livid, Law jumped up and was about to fight until the man pulled out a .45 and aimed in his direction. "You Law right?"

"Who the fuck are you?" Law yelled, spitting blood at his feet. "And why you just hit me?"

The man cocked his weapon. "Answer the fucking question or die. Are you Law Hightower or not?"

Law knew what this was about and felt it best to remain silent. The man was clearly wronged by Kanati and looking to exact revenge on him.

Seeing the fear in Law's eyes, the man smiled, uncocked his weapon and stuffed his gun in the back of his pants. Pulling his shirt down he said, "That nigga killed a boy of mine last night." He pointed at him. "And a lot of dudes looking for you out here. But I know your pops so I'm gonna let you breathe. But I suggest you leave the city or kill yourself. That's your final warning." He walked away, eyes on him the whole time.

Law touched his mouth again and looked at the blood. "Fuck!"

Law was sitting on the porch smoking when his father walked up and looked at his scratched and beaten face. Ever since his beef with Kanati he looked like shit. Standing before his son, Jimmy said, "Is it true?"

"What is it, pop?" He blew out smoke and looked past his father as if he weren't there. "I'm busy."

"Is it true that Sunni was with Kanati first? And that all of this is because of him?"

Law never told his father about Kanati burning down the house or what he was doing in the streets so he was shocked by his inquiry. That's one thing about owning the strip clubs that Law hated. Jimmy found out everything about him, even things he didn't want his father knowing. In his forties, Jimmy's relatively young age had the youngin's respecting him. "I don't know what you mean. Sunni's my bitch."

Taking a deep breath Jimmy said, "A lot of things been happening at my clubs lately. Like strange men asking where you are and where you live." He paused. "I even had a nigga try to follow me to my new house but I was able to shake him off. What's going on? I see you have a busted lip and scratches on your face. Is it because of all of this mess with Kanati?" He paused. "Talk to me, son."

"It's a long story."

"Then shorten it up."

Law sighed. "Go home."

Jimmy cleared his throat. "I'm hearing that Kanati is terrorizing the city and that it's all because of you. And that you burned down his community because he burned down my house. Is this true?"

Wow. This nigga has been hearing a lot of shit. Law thought.

"I'm not gonna lie," Jimmy continued. "If Kanati is doing these things it would surprise me because he is a nice young man and —"

"And what?" He yelled standing up, plucking the lit cigarette past his father's face. "I'm not?" He pointed at himself. "It's obvious you liked him more than me, pops. Ran this dude around town when he stayed with us and even took him to a few of my nigga's cribs. Why?"'

"He was helping me with some things and —,"

"He wasn't your son!" Law pointed to himself. "I am!"

Jimmy looked to the left and back at him. "If it's true that you stole Law's girl and because of it he burned down my house then it's obvious I raised a selfish young man."

Law grinded his teeth. "Wow. Is that the real reason you won't let me and Sunni live in your new house? Because I'm selfish?"

"That's exactly why, Law. I lost enough because of you. Your selfishness has caused you to think that everyone is dumb. And that everyone is naïve like you." He observed him with hate. "But now look at you. You got the girl and you letting her hit and scratch you up. If you think hard can you really say she was worth it?"

Embarrassed, Law flopped down and sighed. His father was right. With each passing day Sunni had become more unhinged and violent. Although he had developed a version of feelings for her at one time it didn't grow into love. This meant he was weighing in on what to do, especially after seeing her run through a balcony door like a lunatic. His mind told him to get rid of her but pride wouldn't let him. And by letting her go Law was essentially saying that the war was for nothing.

"She going through some shit," he removed a cigarette from his pocket. "We gonna be fine though."

Jimmy sighed. "You are a mess, son. Your face. Your spirit. And you wreak of alcohol." He paused. "Plus I can look in your house from where I'm standing and see you not cleaning. That means your girl isn't either." He paused. "Get your life together."

Law continued to look past him. "Even if it means things will get violent?"

"Do what you have to, Law. Just make it go away." He sighed. "Better him than you." He put a firm hand on his shoulder and walked off.

From the open door Sunni saw and heard it all. And when Jimmy drove down the street she pushed the screen door, walked out and crossed her arms over her breasts. It slammed shut. Her face still held a bandage from the glass slicing part of her scalp. "What did he say about me?" She asked as if she didn't know. She mainly wanted to see if he would tell the truth. "Because it's obvious he hates me."

"What you think he said?"

Frowning she walked in front of him. "I'm not going back to Arizona. I'm just not."

"Right now that's the last thing on my mind. This nigga causing more problems than I need out here in these streets." He paused. "So what I don't need is mouth play from you."

"You losing the battle because you not thinking like him." She snatched the cigarette out his hand, walked closer to the edge of the porch and looked outward to the street. "You'll never get Kanati how you're moving." She inhaled and exhaled smoke.

"What you mean?" He frowned.

"When Kanati used to rob people he'd do it from up high. I know it's crazy but him and his friends perfected this technique." She inhaled and exhaled smoke again. "Guess most people don't look up and that gives him the element of surprise." She turned around and glared at him. "Look toward the sky if you wanna find Kanati." She turned back around and faced the street. "It's the only way." She dropped the lit cigarette, smashed it with her bare foot and walked back in the house, the screen door swinging behind her.

CHAPTER THIRTEEN
LAW

Law was jogging as he put major refocus on his life. Starting with stopping the alcoholism, working out and eating better, he vowed to get Kanati no matter what, even though this new energy angered Sunni to no end. She preferred the down and out version of him because he was easy to prey on at his weakest. The new version of Law was different. He was stronger. Wiser.

When his new cell rang he removed it from his sweat pants and answered. "Hello." He leaned on a tree, out of breath.

"You don't know me but I have one question." The caller paused. "Is Kanati's grams still alive?"

"Who are you?" He frowned.

"I am Shilah. A friend of an enemy."

Law took a deep breath.

"Give her to me and I'll call this off. Kanati doesn't know about this but I'm trying to put the drama to bed." He paused. "I'll call you in two hours for your answer. If you choose not to give her up this whole thing will go to the next level. You hold the destiny of the people you love in your hand."

CLICK.

Law looked at Moozy, Petey and L.F. in his living room. Surprisingly Sunni cleaned up when he got back from jogging which shocked the fuck out of him. He figured she was concerned after Jimmy came over that she would be shipped away and to be honest if she didn't get her attitude together Law had plans to do just that.

"They called earlier." Law said to them as he leaned against the wall in the living room. "Well, one of his boy's anyway." He looked at them. "They want the woman."

"Give her to them." Petey said quickly and without hesitation. "Too much shit going down and the city hates you. Relieve the pressure and let these dudes get money again on the streets."

"No." Sunni said walking into the living room. "You'll be a fool if you submit."

Petey shook his head hating the hold she had on him. "You mind if we talk alone, Sunni?" He asked. "This is kind of private."

"Actually I do mind." She paused. "Especially if you talking about releasing hostages and shit." She moved closer to the group. "We've come too far now to let her go."

"We?" Petey said. "You don't know nobody out here."

"You know what I mean."

Petey sighed. "Ten more niggas fell last night, Law. The next part of this plan is the people you know. That means us. Kanati said it himself. Do you really want him to go to that level?" Petey continued. "Do you really want to risk my life? Or your father's?" He paused. "Give her to them. Stop this shit once and for all."

"I hate to say it but I say no too," Moozy said. "Right now she's the only thing keeping you alive." He opened a bag of chips and stuffed a handful in his mouth using his palm as a shovel. "You give that up and you anything out in these streets."

RING.

Law looked at his cell phone sitting on the table.

RING.

Slowly he walked toward it and answered, placing the call on speaker. "Yeah."

"This is Shilah." The caller said. "What's your answer?"

Law looked at Petey, Moozy and L.F. first. Finally his eyes rested on Sunni who shook her head slowly from left to right. Taking a deep breath Law said, "I can't do that."

"Then I will stare down at your friends' cold bodies. And then you will die too."

"What nigga?" Law glared.

CLICK.

Petey shook his head and got up. "One of these days you gotta grow up, man." He said to Law. "And listen to me. At this point you don't even know what you fighting for anymore. You on the verge of losing everything." He paused. "I mean you got the bitch. Ain't that enough?" He walked out, slamming the door behind him.

Sunni walked into L.F.'s basement where Nanni was asleep in the chair, arms still tied behind her back. She had lost a lot of weight but her eyes were still bright with fire.

Approaching slowly, Sunni removed the tie from her mouth and gave her the strawberry shake she held. Thirsty and hungry, Nanni sucked half of it down with small swallows in between.

It was delicious.

"Got enough?" Sunni asked kindly as if she were a friend.

Nanni nodded yes.

Sunni sat the shake on the floor and stood in front of Nanni. Wearing a black long dress, she pulled it over her head and stood completely naked in front of the woman. She wasn't even wearing underwear.

Speaking in her best version of the ancient language Sunni asked, "Why does Kanati not want me?" She paused. "Why did he not fight for me?" She looked down at herself. "Am I that inadequate?"

Nanni gazed at her briefly and turned away.

"What is wrong with me?" Sunni screamed stepping closer. "Tell me now!" Her fists were clenched tightly in knots.

Nanni turned her head the other way.

Angry that Nanni was what she considered disrespecting, she rushed up to her and slapped her face. "LOOK AT ME!"

Nanni slowly turned her head toward her.

"You made him hate me when all I wanted was for Kanati to be strong," Sunni continued. "Like a soldier. Like his parents."

Nanni, despite the circumstances of being held hostage, felt sorry for the sick young woman who only knew her mother and father briefly, and who was eventually sold by her uncle into sexual slavery. It wasn't until her uncle died by an apparent suicide bullet to the brain that she was free. And now due to not knowing who she was her world unraveled before her eyes.

"Kanati wanted you, Sunni," she said in their language. "And you caused all this violence simply because you didn't feel worthy."

"That's not true!"

"I feel sorry for what will become of you, Sunni," Nanni said softly. "I feel sorry because you are too damaged to know what's coming next. And too damaged to know the kind of man you have aroused anger in. Even if years pass and you get happiness, it will be short lived. I promise you."

Sunni glared at her. "Don't feel sorry for me old woman. I'm not the one who won't eat for another two days." She grabbed her dress off the floor and stomped up the stairs.

By T. STYLES

CHAPTER FOURTEEN

MOOZY

Moozy rolled over onto a bag of chips in the spare bed at his brother's house when he heard a noise from afar.

It sounded like a whistle.

Since Kanati and his crew were on the hunt, he figured living there would make him safe. Could he be wrong? Thinking he was hearing things, the moment his face hit the pillow he was out again, until he heard someone yell. Opening his eyes he tried to focus on the sound but things were silent in that moment. He almost drifted back to sleep again until...

"MOOZY!"

Afraid, Moozy leapt up and ran toward the back of the house where his brother slept. Out of breath due to his weight, he was barely able to push the door open. But when he did he was immediately brought to his knees when Micco stole him in the jaw.

He didn't even know he was there.

From the floor, holding his face Moozy looked across the room and to the bed in front of him. Sitting on top of the headboard was Kanati, with Shilah standing to the left and Bidzil to the right, both holding knives. His brother lie on the mattress between Kanati's feet.

Moozy immediately wanted to kill himself when he saw his brother's beaten pummeled face. Lewis was his best friend and he couldn't believe he brought this heat to his door. If only he had listened to Petey and convinced Law to let the old woman go maybe this would not be his fate.

"Listen, man," Moozy stood on his knees, preparing to get up until he was struck again.

"Say everything you gotta from down there," Micco said, pointing a stiff finger his way. "I'm not fucking around."

"Who are these dudes?" Lewis yelled to his brother. "What's going on, Moozy? Say something!"

Moozy held his bloodied lip not believing Micco could hit so hard. "I'm sorry, Lew." Moozy said. "I'm so fucking sorry."

"We didn't have to come to this," Kanati said calmly. "We didn't want to do this shit but you and your friends violated."

"Us?" Moozy said, tears running down his face. "You burned Law's house down! All of this is on you!"

"Burned down Law's house?" Kanati frowned. "That's a fucking lie!"

Moozy didn't know if he was trying to save face or not in front of his friends so he left the matter alone. Besides, it wouldn't help his situation anyway. "Listen, I don't want to do any of this. I'm just—"

"Is my grandmother alive?"

"Come on, Kanati," Moozy said looking at his brother and everyone present as if trying to convince a jury of his peers. "Why you doing this to me? Law's the one who stole your girl. I ain't have nothing to do with that shit."

"Is my grandmother alive or not?"

"I don't know, man," Moozy lied, knowing she was in the basement of L.F.'s trashed out house. But the last thing he wanted was to be the one to lead them there only to meet his fate regardless. "I swear I don't. You know how Law be. He does what he wants." He looked at his brother who was trembling. Although 32 he was a small time dealer who wasn't as deep in the streets as Moozy so guilt weighed heavily on Moozy's heart. "Please don't hurt him."

"It's too bad you don't know if she's alive," Kanati said as he slowly brought the knife across his brother's neck, opening the flesh in front of him. When Moozy passed out after seeing Lewis's blood pour onto the sheets under his body Micco slapped him awake.

"Tell Law his time has run out," Kanati said. "I'm coming for him soon."

Frantic, Moozy kicked in the front door of Law's house, a letter V was cut into his head.

Thinking his time on earth was over, Law busted out of his bedroom and sent a bullet whizzing by Moozy's head, believing Kanati had finally made good on his promise.

"It's me, man!" Moozy yelled having ducked just in time. "Don't shoot!"

"What the fuck you doing then?" Law turned on the light and looked at his door hanging off the hinges and aimed at him again. Besides, how did he know he wasn't out to get him? "Fuck is wrong with you? Why you do that to my door?" He paused. "And what happened to your face?"

By T. STYLES

"That nigga killed my brother, man," he yelled, blood pouring into his eyes due to the letter V on his forehead. "He killed my brother and it's all your fault."

Law lowered the weapon and flopped on the edge of his sofa, taking a deep breath. "I'm sorry, Moo."

"I want this nigga gone!" He cried louder pacing wildly in front of him. "Do you hear me? I want this nigga gone!"

Law wiped his hand down his face. "I got some things in motion. Trust me." He looked at his door. "But you gonna pay to get my door fixed."

Kanati looked out the window while Tammi drove him and his crew down the street on the way to the motel. When they pulled over at a McDonalds, everyone but Kanati and Tammi got out. "Kanati, what do you and your, um friends do? I mean for a living."

He sighed. "What I tell you about asking questions?" He looked out the window at the McDonalds.

"I'm just asking because, well, the blood." She pointed to his jeans. "And I guess I'm just worried about you that's all."

"Stay out of it, Tammi." He sighed and looked at the restaurant.

"Actually I can't stay out of it, since we, well, you know." She looked at him and smiled. "Fucked and all."

"Tammi—"

"I know, I know, the language," she paused after cutting him off. "For real, Kanati, I got a bad feeling that something is going to happen tonight." He looked at her and she realized she had his entire attention. "And I feel like I gotta tell you to be careful. But there's a reason."

Micco, Shilah and Bidzil trudged into their motel room barely picking up their feet they were so exhausted. Paris after waiting hours for their return was relieved when he saw them. Pushing out of his car he rushed into his motel room. Once the door was locked, inside the dark room he walked up to the window and pushed the grungy yellow curtains aside while looking out.

From inside he peered across the street at his prey's room. He was so excited he could hardly contain himself. Besides, the city was looking for the men and he had sights on them. This could not only net big money but it could also be enough to get himself out of Maryland because the payout would be huge, over ninety thousand dollars to be exact. A bunch of Baltimore's finest trap execs had pooled their funds together all to see Kanati's reign come to an end and it looked like Paris alone was gonna secure the bag.

Removing the cell from his pocket he made a call. "Tone, it's Paris. Where you at?"

"Don't worry about all that, nigga." He paused. "They back or not? I been waiting all day on your call."

"Yep," he looked out the window again. He could see Shilah going back and forth to Tammi's van. "Got my money though?"

"I do but that pretty nigga better be there." He paused. "The payout ain't gonna be yours unless we get him. What's the address?"

That's when it dawned on Paris that he hadn't seen Kanati. Pushing the curtains aside wider he looked at the motel room again and then the van. Maybe Kanati was inside and he couldn't see him. "Yeah, where are you?" He whispered to himself, although the phone was still in his hand.

"I'm here," Kanati said from behind.

Horrified, Paris dropped the phone, turned around and tried to run but Kanati slammed his hand over his mouth and brought the blade across his throat. He held onto him until he stopped wiggling, while feeling his spirit leave this world.

Dead, Kanati watched him drop to the floor and bent down to wipe the blood off his knife and onto Paris's pants.

That was a close call. He thought.

Had Tammi not seen Paris take pictures when Shilah, Bidzil and Micco got out the cab that one morning him and his friends would be after thoughts. At first she thought seeing Paris take the pictures wasn't a big deal but she thought it was best to tell him anyway.

She had proved more and more that she was down for him. If only he hadn't been wronged before he could trust her more fully. And yet something in his spirit told him she was lying but he couldn't put his finger on how or about what.

Had Sunni not fucked up his mind he would probably go with his emotions and consider taking things to the next level. But if history had proven one thing to him it was that some women could not be trusted.

With Paris dead to rights, Kanati slowly walked out of the motel room. Shilah and his crew approached him when he walked across the parking lot. Hopeful, Shilah looked over Kanati's shoulder at Paris's open door. "It's done?"

Kanati nodded.

Shilah sighed in relief.

"Heard the nigga in the act of selling us out and everything," Kanati continued. "We still need to get another room though, just to be sure."

Shilah took a deep breath and ran his hand down his face. "It'll be the third one in less than a week. Things are getting tighter now, K. But it's better safe than sorry."

"Indeed. So lets finish them off. I'm ready to go home too."

Tammi was on her phone on the side of the motel room when Kanati walked up behind her. Before approaching he hung back to hear what she was saying. Why didn't she want to talk in her car? Or the room? *There she was with the sneaky shit again.* He thought. Between the phone calls in the bathroom and the secret texting that went on for minutes at a time, something told him she was foul.

Or maybe she was in a relationship and had been lying about it the whole time. But if that were true, and she had a man, what could he do? Kanati made it clear that he wasn't interested in being exclusive. More than that, he barely said two words to her when they were alone, afraid to open up fully.

When Tammi heard Kanati behind her, and saw he was about to walk away she said into the phone, "I'll call you back." Dumping her phone into her pocket she moved quickly toward him. "Everything okay?"

He turned around and faced her. The veins in his neck pulsating. "Yeah."

She nodded. "So, uh, where are we driving tonight?"

"Who was that?" He paused unable to hide his emotions. "On the phone?" The moment he asked he felt like a sucker. But he was feeling her and needed some answers.

She frowned a little. "Wait...but I thought we weren't doing that."

He looked down because she called him out. Nodding slowly he said, "Yeah, you right." He cleared his throat. "It ain't my business to ask you yours so let's leave it at that. But listen, we won't be needing you to drive us around no more." Kanati turned and attempted to walk away when she grabbed his hand.

"But, why, what's wrong?" Her wide eyes peered into his. "I said I'm with you no matter what? Why has that changed?"

"We gonna get a car. Don't need you no more."

"Kanati," she said softly pushing him up against the cold brick wall. "Don't do this." She wrapped her arms around his waist and tried to lay her head on his chest but he pushed her back slowly. "Please talk to me."

"Quit all this extra shit!" He yelled down at her. "Now start the fucking van." He pointed over her head. "We leaving!" He stormed off.

CHAPTER FIFTEEN

KANATI

Kanati took the first step on the right side of a brownstone in Baltimore when he missed a step and fell down. Luckily Bidzil, Shilah and Micco were below and able to catch him. If not he would've hit the concrete and at the very least broken an ankle or leg.

"What's up with you tonight?" Shilah whispered, as the others looked to be sure no one was coming. "You been acting different since we left the new motel."

Kanati wiped his hand down his face. He felt stupid for letting yet another woman into his mental sphere but there he was, forced to deal with the truth. He was falling in love with a stranger. "I'm fine." He turned around and faced the wall. "Just be on the look out."

"He's coming," Micco whispered, rushing up to Kanati and Shilah. "We have to hurry up and get into position."

"Then move," Kanati instructed. "I'm good."

Kanati quickly climbed along side the house, using the window ledges as steps as Bidzil moved toward the other side of the home preparing to do the same. Micco and Shilah stayed on ground level where they could see whoever entered or left the premises.

On top of the brownstone, Kanati was waiting for the whistle that one of his friends would give below, indicating that their mark was out front. But his mind was inundated with life again.

First he thought about Nanni and wondered if it were truly possible for her to be alive. Then he thought about his community in Arizona and the shame he felt for bringing an outsider under their roof only to destroy what they built. And finally he thought about Tammi and the fact that in a short period of time she had captured his heart.

"Stay focused, Kanati," he said to himself sitting on the roof and looking downward. "Stay focused."

L.F. exited his car with his cell phone pressed against his ear. He was loud and obnoxious and adding unnecessary volume to the quietness that Kanati and his crew preferred to operate under.

By T. STYLES

L.F. closed his car door. "Nigga, I'm telling you I'm coming," L.F. said loudly into his phone before activating his alarm on his black Benz. "If you heard me then why the fuck you keep asking?" He walked up the steps leading to his house and removed his keys. "Yeah, I'm bringing him too."

Once he trotted up the steps he was now hidden under the cover of the awning so Kanati could no longer hear or see him from above. Just that quickly he went radio silent. Had Kanati not been in his head he would have noticed the awning at first and changed the plans.

But the issues were now many.

First off he knew that his crew was waiting on the whistle he blew, indicating that it was time to move forward on the plan. But since L.F. was quiet and out of view he couldn't tell if he was inside or outside the house. Not only that but Bidzil was supposed to come up through the front door once Kanati came through the window for support after the whistle was made. This would give Shilah and Micco the time they needed to add additional protection by rushing into L.F.'s crib.

But now that he couldn't hear or see L.F., this made shit beyond difficult to access. Kanati had excellent senses so normally this wouldn't be a problem. He could hear further than a lot of people. See better than most and was stronger than many. But all of that went out the window once love got involved.

Tiring of waiting, a minute later Bidzil climbed on the side of the wall. "What's going on?" He whispered. "Is he inside or —"

BOOM! BOOM! BOOM!

Before Kanati and Bidzil knew what happened several rounds of bullets flew from an adjacent window across the street. When Kanati looked in the direction he saw two shooters unleashing bullets at them. Very nimble, he was able to climb down the side quickly and run into the street to prevent getting hit.

"Let's bounce!" Kanati yelled, which alerted Micco and Shilah who were waiting in their positions. Bidzil was also running behind them, at full speed.

Hearing the bullets, and thinking on her feet, Tammi had the car running and met them closer than where they originally planned. Her smart and quick move definitely saved Kanati's life. When everyone was in the van she pressed the gas with all her might, almost breaking her toes due to the pressure.

An approaching light turned red but she wasn't going to stop no matter what. Besides there were two cars behind her that were moving toward them quickly. Tammi's eyes were wide and her chest rose heavily up and down as she looked for a way out.

She was feeling faint.

Seeing this, placing a hand calmly on top of the one that held the gearshift, Kanati looked over at her. She looked at him and slowly relaxed despite being somewhat nervous. With his hand on top of hers he moved his index finger right and she went right. When an unrelated car got in the way he moved his index finger left and she took a left into an alley.

Looking behind him Kanati almost lost the tip of his nose when a bullet came flying into the back window and through the front window. Sending glass shattering everywhere. Now the culprits were lighting Tammi's ride up with fire. "Damn, these mothafuckas won't let us be!" Micco yelled.

"From here on out we gotta use guns!" Shilah said. "Shit serious now."

"You know how I feel about guns," Kanati said. Ever since his parents died due to guns in the military he always had a dis-taste for firepower. But still there was something to be said to the old adage. Never bring a knife to a gunfight and Kanati and his crew were finding that out the hard way. They were in Baltimore.

And the weapon of choice was always a hammer.

"We have to now," Shilah said. "Let's just hope we make it out alive." The cars were some ways back from Kanati's gang but they could hear them approaching.

Focusing on the front Kanati saw that their light was about to turn red and that two tractor-trailers were at the intersection before them preparing to move when their light turned green. If Tammi drove in front of them it was a possibility that the tractors would crash into them, killing everyone inside. And yet if they sat where they were they would be annihilated. So the moment the light turned red Kanati yelled, "Go!"

Without question she took off and rolled behind the first tractor-trailer, missing it by inches. The cars holding the gunmen took off behind them also but the second tractor trailer dipped in front of them, causing the shooters to crash into it's side.

Micco looked behind them at the wreckage and the flames. "Yes!" He cheered. "You did that shit!" He said to Tammi putting a hand on her shoulder.

Tammi grinned at Micco and looked over at Kanati. "I can't believe I got us away."

Kanati looked behind them and back at her. "Well believe it! You just saved our lives." He looked at her and gripped her hand tighter. "Thank you."

"Kanati, stop the car," Shilah said softly.

"Nah, we need more room between us just in case they send somebody else."

"You gotta stop now, man," Shilah persisted. "I'm serious."

"Okay." Kanati nodded and Tammi pulled into an alley to get the van off the street and out of view. "What is it, man? We have—" Kanati's sentence stopped in his throat when he saw Bidzil in the back with his eyes closed, blood pouring out of his gut. Feeling as if the world was spinning, Kanati frantically pushed out of the van and opened the back door.

Everyone else piled out too.

Kanati eased inside, hoping it wasn't true. "Bid, wake up, man," Kanati said softly touching his arm. "Bid, get the fuck up." He wouldn't budge, instead his head rocked slightly every time he shoved him. "Get up, man!" He pushed him harder. "Get up!"

"Kanati, stop," Shilah said rushing behind him, wrapping his arms around his waist and pulling. "He gone, man! He gone!"

Devastated, Kanati got out of the car slowly, put both of his hands on his head and screamed, "NOOOO!!!!!" He dropped to his knees.

When his cell phone rang Kanati reached into his pocket and took it out. Pushing the button he answered. "For future reference maybe you should stay off them rooftops," Sunni said sarcastically as Law and his friends laughed in the background.

Devastated and defeated, Kanati tossed the phone and it slammed into the wall, crashing into several pieces. His friends, including Tammi walked up to him and awaited his word. "I want everything he loves to bleed!" Kanati said softly. "Starting tonight!"

CHAPTER SIXTEEN
LAW

Law, Moozy, L.F. and Petey were in Law's father's new house in the basement, giddy about their win. Sunni was also present and sitting on the sofa drinking a glass of wine. Jimmy had just recently moved in so he didn't have the luxuries he was accustomed to at his old house just yet but he was working on it for sure.

But the emptiness of the house suited Law's purposes just fine, especially since they were only discussing business.

"...So this nigga was really crawling up the wall," L.F. said laughing hysterically. "And I'm like, I know I'm not actually seeing this shit from my peripheral. At the same time I can't say shit because I'm supposed to be faking on this phone."

Law and Moozy busted out into laughter.

"But it's a good thing I moved his grandmother to that other spot like you said, Petey." L.F. continued. "He would've lucked up and found that bitch." He paused. "How the fuck he know where I lived anyway?"

"My father used to take him with him to drop shit off to yah for me," Law said. "And the nigga must've remembered the addresses."

"I really can't believe he was crawling up the side of the house," L.F. laughed harder.

"I told you the boy super human," Moozy laughed, eating a subway sandwich with so much vinegar it stank every time he talked. "I use to see him going up them trees at Jimmy's old house all the time."

"He's not super human," Sunni said taking a large sip of wine while pouring another glass from the bottle on the table. "He's just creative. And smarter than you all." She sat the bottle down and took another sip.

Law frowned at her. "You sound like you still got it in for this nigga or something."

"Me?" She pointed at herself. "Your crew the ones who act like he can't be brought down. If it breathes it can bleed."

Law shook his head. Lately every time she opened her mouth she irritated him but what could he do?

"So what now?" Petey asked. "Because this is far from over. If anything we angered him even more after this."

"Like he said you guys are next," Law continued. "We saw that when he tried to move on L.F. So I think

168   **By T. STYLES**

everybody needs to keep their eyes open and stay some place else other than your crib."

Moozy dropped his sandwich out of his hand and picked it up off the floor. Everyone silently waited to see if he would bite it.

He did.

"Gross, Moo," L.F. said.

"What?" He asked raising his hand. "His pops just moved in. The floor still clean and shit."

Everyone shook their heads.

"Be careful," Law said to all of them while returning to the subject at hand. "Don't make no moves you don't have to out in these streets. To be honest I don't think we have to do anything but wait for him to come to us."

"I just be glad when this shit is done," Moozy said. "I got a scar for life behind this shit. He ate the remainder of his sandwich and pointed at the bandage on his head, as if niggas didn't already see the bloodied stank mess. "Not to mention this nigga took my brother from me. I suffered enough."

"What about his grandmother?" Petey asked.

Law sighed. "How come every time we get together you bringing that up?" He paused. "Just let it go."

"Is she alive?"

"Yeah, man." Law snapped. "Why wouldn't she be? You heard L.F. say he had her moved."

Petey shrugged. "I just feel like the best thing to get this nigga away from Baltimore is to give him back his peoples." He paused. "And I know you got your feelings on the matter but I really believe some of us ain't gonna live to talk about shit later if we don't hand her over. And now."

"And I already said I'm not doing that." Law snapped. "You act like saying it in a different way gonna change how I feel. It's not happening."

Petey sighed. "Look, man, can I talk to you in private?"

Law shook his head no.

"Please."

Law looked around and took a deep breath. "Everybody bounce."

"Me too?" Sunni asked.

"Yeah." When everyone was gone Petey sat on the sofa and Law sat across from him in the recliner. "Now what is it?"

"I got it on good authority that Sunni lied."

He frowned. "About what?"

"Who burned down your pop's house. I think it was her."

"How you sound?" He laughed once. "If Kanati didn't do it then why would she?"

Petey shrugged. "I don't know." He paused. "Maybe the girl is bananas." He paused. "After all, she did run into the balcony door. Or are we gonna just pretend like that didn't happen?"

He frowned. "Fuck would she do that for?"

"Listen, like I said the broad is crazy, man. And I know you not feeling that, or can even understand it but it don't mean it's not true. I mean, how can we be sure she didn't?"

"Because she didn't have a reason."

"She does have a reason." Petey threw his hands up. "All of this." Petey paused. "As much as I hate to admit it some women feel stronger when a war starts because of them. Maybe she's one of them."

Law ran his hand down his face and then sat up, placing his arms on his knees and then clasping his hands together. "She had a chance to be with him. And she chose me. It doesn't make sense that she would burn down my family's house just to get back at him. She loved that place too much."

"Look, man, I could be wrong but what if I'm not?"

VILLAINS: IT'S SAVAGE SEASON   171

He shook his head. "Listen, I want to tell you something." He exhaled. "She's pregnant."

Petey felt as if a boulder fell on his dick. "No, no, no, bruh. You didn't connect with her for life did you? Why?"

Law frowned. "How you sound? I tell you I'm expecting a kid and you yell no."

"Don't you see...now you in too deep." Petey pleaded. "Ain't no turning back now unless you can get her to make the pregnancy go away."

"I'm gonna pretend like you didn't say that." He paused. "Now I'ma ask you this...are you my friend or not?"

"You know I am."

"Good, because if something happened to me I need you to look after her like you looking after me, especially while she's pregnant with my kid. And that's the bottom line."

"Well that brings me to my next point." Petey sighed deeply. "Please, please consider letting his grandmother go. If you got a family on the way the last thing you need is all this. Just consider it, Law. Okay?"

As they continued to talk neither knew that Sunni was hiding in the bathroom, with the door slightly cracked, ear hustle on a million.

Moozy walked to his car with three number 5's from *Chicken Fast* and they were all for him. Instead of staying out the way like Law commanded, he did the exact opposite making a fast food run an hour. When he opened the car door he tossed the bags into the passenger seat and slid inside. His mouth watered as he thought about the dirty things he was about to do to his food. To be honest he was not at his best unless he was eating at least twenty times a day.

As he pushed the button on his alarm to unlock his pick up truck, he was about to pull off when a hand slammed against his forehead, pressing the bandage already present. When he looked in the rearview mirror and saw Kanati's eyes, he knew it was over.

"Please don't do this, man," Moozy whispered, peeing in his seat.

"Too late," Kanati replied as he slid the knife across his neck, deeper than normal, almost severing his head. "That was for my nigga Bid." He spit in his hair. "Die slow bitch!"

CHAPTER SEVENTEEN

KANATI

ONE WEEK LATER

Kanati walked up to a house he was renting from an elderly man in Reisterstown Maryland. He was about to enter when he saw Tammi standing on the side of the house, waiting for him. Had it been Law he would've been dead and he knew it. "Where you been, Kanati?" She asked. "I been waiting for you. Worried. And concerned."

He took a deep breath. "How you find me?" He unlocked the door.

"I told you about this place remember? That's how I knew about it." She moved closer. "But where have you been? And why haven't you called?" He walked inside and she stood in the doorway. "Can I come inside? Please?"

He nodded yes and she followed, closing the door behind her. As she looked around from where she stood she noticed the house was old but neat. The furniture, made of harsh burlap type material, was soiled because of time but still in tact. The wooden table in the center of the living room was chipped but again, still useable. On the side of the sofa were a pillow, blankets and sheets neatly folded and stacked and Tammi figured he slept there instead of the bedroom.

Kanati sat down on the sofa and sighed. "What you want, Tammi?"

"You." She sat next to him and placed her hand on his leg. "Kanati, where were you?"

"We had to bury Bid and Micco's mom." He exhaled. "So I went back to Arizona for a little while to take care of that."

She removed her hand. "Oh yeah, that's right, I'm very sorry."

He nodded. "Me too."

"Where are Micco and Shilah?" She looked around. "In the back?"

"Nah. They in Arizona."

She took a deep breath. "They didn't want to be involved in all of this no more right? Whatever this is?"

"Something like that." He looked at her. "Listen, I was wrong for involving you in my shit. And even though I can't tell you what's happening, I want you to know I'm never gonna put you in that type of situation again."

"But I'm already involved, Kanati." She moved closer and now their legs touched. "I'm already involved because I fell in love with you. And now I worry about you too. And I know I'm not as pretty as Sunni and —"

He grabbed her wrist and yanked her upwards, both of them now on their feet. "How the fuck you know about Sunni?"

She frowned and looked at the firm grasp he held on her. "Kanati, you're hurting me."

He squeezed tighter leaving finger indentions in her skin. "How the fuck you know 'bout her?"

"I heard Micco and Shilah talking about her one night at the motel." She winced in pain. "Now please let me go."

He released her and flopped back down. "I'm sorry." He ran both hands down his face. "Please forgive me. But this is why I don't want you around. The way shit moves in my mind I can't say how regular I would be from one moment to the next. Mentally I'm done and if you stay with me you may not be safe."

"And I don't care about you being normal." She sat next to him. "I just want you to talk to me, Kanati. With no judgment I swear."

He shook his head. "I had a bad life back in Arizona." He took a deep breath. "My father lived on the reservation all his life and then when he became a citizen off the reservation to have a chance at a better life, he met my mother in the US army and married her. I always felt like something was different when I was growing up on the barracks but we spent so much of our time involved with other families that I let it go.

"Well when my parents died the army shipped me back to stay on the reservation with my Nanni but I hated everything and everybody. I didn't know my family and the first niggas I connected with were Bid, Shilah and Micco." He chuckled once. "And we stayed in trouble, trust me. Robbed a few dudes off the reservation and some more shit I can never speak about to you. I got money any way I could and just lived hard.

"But my grandmother was always so loving and supportive," he continued. "Never judged me and it made me want to change." He shrugged. "So I decided to try to be a better version of me, especially after I got the girl I thought would look good on my arm. Before long I cleaned up my life and I thought it was because of Sunni."

"Wow…you changed because of her." She looked down at her fingers. "That's nice." She was ill with jealousy.

"I guess." He shrugged. "Eventually I got off the streets and stayed off. My friends bucked at first but after awhile they changed a little too. And if they were involved in crime they kept it off the reservation and I didn't know about it. And then what happens?" He frowned. "My bitch leaves with the first dude I bring into the picture and everything gets fucked up. Now I wonder if she ever wanted me to go straight. I always assumed she did but now that I think about it, I believe Sunni wanted the fast life so I could take her off the reservation. She always hated it."

"Did you love her?"

He looked at her. "No."

Her eyebrows rose. "Wait…you didn't love her?"

"Nah." He shook his head. "I mean, at first I thought I was supposed to be in love because everybody but my friends and grandmother kept telling me I was lucky. And like I said I was trying to go on the straight and narrow so I chose her but…she was a real mean person. Had a lot of stuff going on that I thought I could change. Turns out I couldn't."

"Wow." She paused. "So you not here fighting for her?"

He laughed and grabbed the remote off the table. "Not even close." He turned the TV on and sat back, tossing the remote down. "Didn't think I could feel for somebody else until…"

Her eyes widened. "Until?"

Kanati's gaze was now glued on the TV and he sat up straight, giving all of his attention to the program. Suddenly he couldn't hear her anymore if he tried.

"Until?" She repeated, hoping he'd finally claim his love for her. "Kanati, what were you about to say?"

"Hold up," he said picking up the remote again and turning the sound up high.

As the newscaster spoke he couldn't believe his eyes or ears. They were reporting on several sexual assaults that happened in Baltimore city. What got the community concerned about the string of rapes were not only the crimes but also the letter V that was placed on the thigh of every woman impacted.

Kanati was devastated that his mark was being used for something so atrocious and he didn't see copycats coming when he planned Law's demise. Standing up he continued to look at the TV as guilt weighed on him even more. He would never hurt a woman in such a vile way.

Tammi stood up. "Kanati, is everything okay?"

"No."

"Well can I do anything?" She looked at him and then the television still unsure of what was happening.

"Nah, I just have to move on my plans sooner than I thought." He paused. "I'll talk to you later, Tammi."

"But I wanted to stay with you and—"

"Tammi, just go!" He pointed behind her at the door. "Now!"

She was about to leave when he walked up behind her, grabbed her softly and kissed her cheek. "I'm a fucked up man so you gotta forgive me." He paused. "I just can't have something else happening to another person I love." He kissed her again and walked away.

She got her answer.

CHAPTER EIGHTEEN

SUNNI

Law was lying in bed jerking off in a motel room. He was just about to cum when Sunni rolled over full of attitude and asked, "What you doing?"

He sighed and rolled his eyes. "Nothing now."

"Then why the bed moving up and down?"

"Okay, if you must know I was beating my dick."

She sat up, turned the light on and crossed her arms over her chest. "What is wrong with you? How come you don't want to touch me but you can beat your dick in our bed? How come whenever I'm around you I feel ugly?"

"You gotta ask your mama that."

"Excuse me!" She yelled.

He shrugged, pushed his dick back into his boxers, shoved the covers aside and sat on the edge of the bed. "I'm gonna be real with you, this ain't working. I know you pregnant and I'm gonna do right by you but I gotta be honest. We may not be able to rock together anymore."

She placed her hand on her chest. "But why?"

"Because since you been here I lost everything, Sunni. And I'm starting to wonder if it was worth it."

Stunned, she eased off the bed and stood in front of him. "So you're blaming me for all this? Even though I was the one who told you how to get Kanati?"

He shrugged. "I don't know why I blame you." He glared at her. "But tell me something, do I have a reason?"

She crossed her arms over her chest. "Say what you mean, Law. Because it's obvious you holding back on something."

He took a deep breath. "Okay." He clapped his hands together once. "Did you burn my pops house down?"

"Me?" Her arms dropped at her sides. "Why would I do something like that?"

"I don't know. That's why I'm asking."

"Kanati burned that house down because he was mad that you took me away from him." She moved closer to him. "So if anybody is to blame it's you. Don't put this shit on me."

"It's mighty funny he didn't ask for you once since he been here."

Silence.

He laughed. "If only I could go back in time to that day I went to Arizona," he continued. "I should've let your ass stay right where you were."

"You know what, fuck you!" She stormed to the bathroom and slammed the door.

"Fuck!" He said to himself. "I can't be with this bitch no more." He continued. "She driving me crazy."

Law slipped into his clothing and was about to leave the motel for a breather when all of a sudden he heard small thuds. When he walked to the bathroom he discerned what sounded like Sunni expelling a lot of air as if she was being hit. When he turned the knob he saw her slamming her fists into her stomach multiple times.

"What are you doing, fool?" He asked rushing inside, knocking the doorknob into the wall behind it. "Why you hitting yourself?" He grabbed at her hands but she started hitting her face instead. "I'm sick of this wacko shit! You hear me? Done with it!"

"I hate me! I hate me! I hate me!" She punched herself so many times her lips started bleeding. "I hate this baby too! I hate this baby too!"

It took extreme strength but before long he was able to get a hold of her from behind and stop her from injuring herself more.

When Law saw that Sunni was asleep in the bed he walked outside where Petey was smoking a cigarette looking at the horizon as the sun went down in a show of orange and purple. "Let me be the first to say, you were right, man."

Petey smiled. "About what?" He knew what he meant but he wanted to hear the words.

"I should've left that bitch right where she was. In Arizona." He whispered. "She crazy, man. Fucking crazy."

Petey smiled, dropped the cigarette, smashed it with his shoe and looked over at him. "That's life." He shrugged. "We all want what we can't have and when we get it we realize it ain't changing shit. We still the same niggas we were before we got *the thing* we thought we couldn't live without. Just bogged down more by it that's all."

"What am I going to do?"

"I don't know," Petey shrugged. "She's pregnant. You in it for the long run now."

Law leaned against the column and looked outward at the sunset. "What about his grandmother? Should we give her to him now?"

"Before they killed Moo I would've said yes. I made my position clear and you know it." Petey shrugged. "But now I think giving her up will make shit worse. I think we need to hold onto her for a little. Make some demands after we make shit hot for them first."

"We already did that when we killed one of his boys."

"Yeah, and they came back and got Moo." He paused. "That means the next move is on us."

Law wiped his hand down his face. "Fuck!" He yelled. "I mean, maybe the nigga gone back home. It's been over a week and I haven't heard anything except about them rapes."

"He not doing no shit like that," Petey said. "Ain't in his makeup."

"I know." He paused. "I just think he's done and gone back that's all."

"You just don't get it do you?" Petey paused. "Men like Kanati don't start things they don't finish. Now I don't know why he quiet all of a sudden but he ain't letting up until you dead. Trust me. I can still feel him in the city."

Law nodded. "I need to get some air. Can you keep an eye on Sunni for me."

"I got you." Petey dapped him. "But be careful, man. I don't trust tonight for some reason. It feels sinister."

"Man, that bitch ain't calling me back," David said as he and Law bopped to his car. David disarmed the alarm and slid into the driver's seat of his Honda Accord while Law slipped into the passenger's. They just left a small lounge off the map in Virginia and were headed to get something to eat.

Hanging with him was the best time Law had in weeks.

"I told you that when I saw her talking to the nigga before you earlier tonight, but what can I say?" Law said.

David laughed a few times and removed his cell phone from his pocket. "So what you wanna eat?"

"Anything," Law said grabbing his cell too. "I ain't ate good in two days."

David continued to text intensely and Law suddenly felt weird. The hairs on the back of his neck stood up. He looked over at him and back at his own phone wondering who he was hitting and why so serious all of a sudden. Law couldn't put his finger on it but something felt off and he felt eerie.

"What you say, man?" David asked Law although he hadn't said a mumbling word in over a minute. "I ain't hear you."

"Nothing." Law frowned. Something was definitely up.

"Oh, I thought I —"

BOOM!

Going with his instincts, Law fired into David's stomach with a hot ball of lead. And he was smart too because David had his free hand on a gun in his compartment on the door and was just about to kill Law for the trouble of the city. He was sick of the drama in the streets courtesy of Kanati and wanted to put an end to it, thereby becoming a hero and a legend in the same right. Instead he got a bullet to the gut for his valor.

"Wow, nigga," Law said to the dying man. "You were about to kill me?"

David could barely talk with blood filling up in his mouth but was able to say, "It was just business."

"Just business?" Law frowned before shooting him again in the chest. Pushing the door open and then running into the night, he left it open and the bell dinging.

By T. STYLES

CHAPTER NINETEEN

LAW

Law hung in the corner smoking a cigarette nervously on a city street in Virginia waiting for a ride. His hand shook as he exhaled and inhaled the smoke. It was his fifth jack of the hour. He couldn't believe a man he considered a friend would try to kill him just because trap niggas were mad that he brought unnecessary heat to the streets. Besides, he wasn't the culprit.

Kanati was!

After twenty minutes of severe chain-smoking that could've landed him in a hospital, a gold Infiniti truck finally pulled up. He dropped the cigarette and slipped quickly into the passenger seat. "Thanks, Vanessa." He locked the door and looked in the back and then at her. "I really 'ppreciate this, man." The nicotine had him geeking.

She sighed. "No problem."

He looked out the windows as if he were being followed. "I can't believe this shit's happening."

She laughed once.

"What was that for?" He asked.

"You always had a way of only seeing what you want to see." She paused. "And now it finally came back to haunt you." She shook her head. "Even showcased that exotic whore all over the city and for what? Trouble."

"So you still mad at me after all this time huh?"

"Yep, I'm always mad at you, Law," she paused as she continued to drive down the street and onto the beltway leading back to Baltimore. "You broke my heart but it doesn't mean I don't love you."

"Listen, we couldn't be the way you wanted us to be, Vanessa." He paused. "We tried and it didn't work."

She laughed. "But why not? Because I didn't have real hair rolling down my back or a tiny nose?"

"No." He took a deep breath. "It's because I...you know what...I don't even know."

She sighed. "I know what the answer is, Law. You don't even have to lie. You only want women that don't belong to you. Just like you pulled me from Magic C before he got killed, you did the same thing to Kanati with Sunni. It's like you don't feel good about yourself unless you taking what another man has. I mean when is it all gonna stop? When can you be grateful for your own?"

"You see, this is why I didn't want you picking me up," he pointed at her. "You always be on this dumb shit."

She shrugged and pulled over on the shoulder of the highway. "Well let me remedy that right now." When the car was parked she hit the unlock button she said, "There you go. Bounce, my nigga."

He took a deep breath. "Listen, man, I'm sorry."

"For what, Law?" She crossed her arms over her chest.

He shrugged. "For everything." He paused. "You think if I couldn't drop that bitch back off in Arizona I wouldn't?"

"So why don't you?" She said turning to face him. "She caused too much drama since she been here. Let her go."

He looked at her and flopped back in the seat, staring ahead of him. "I can't because she pregnant."

"Wow..." she sighed. "You went there."

"To be honest I don't even know how it happened." He said. "I barely fucked that bitch."

"All it takes is a little bit of nut, you know that."

"Apparently so." He sighed deeply. "My dick too strong for my own good." He looked down at it. "DAMN YOU!"

He looked at her and they both broke out into heavy laughter. When they simmered down she locked the doors and pulled off again. "This is my problem." She took a deep breath.

"What's that?"

"I can never stay mad at you."

He nodded. "You may not want to hear what I'm about to say but it's the truth. The best thing I could've done was stay out of your life. I know you wanted to be together but I'm bad luck, V. That's on mothers. Everybody's life I touch I fuck up. And I don't know how to stop."

"Start with treating people how you want to be treated, Law." She paused. "How 'bout you start there and watch things change for the better."

Jimmy just finished mowing his lawn when he stepped back into the house and saw Kanati sitting on the counter holding a gun in his direction. His eyes widened and then he lowered his head as he took a deep breath. He was done for and he knew it. "So

By T. STYLES

there's nothing I can do huh?" Jimmy asked. "To get you to spare my life?"

"Nah. I'm done giving favors out in these streets. Your boy took too much from me."

Jimmy took another deep breath. "You mind if I make us a drink?"

"Not thirsty."

"Please, man," Jimmy said. "I know my son did some things that didn't sit with you, but for the most part I always did good by you, right? I mean, wouldn't you agree?" He paused. "Give a dying man his fill."

Kanati nodded.

Jimmy opened the refrigerator and grabbed the ice trays and the vodka from the freezer. "You know, I understand why you doing all of this." He closed the fridge and popped ice into two glasses. "I always told my son the past would come back asking questions." He poured vodka into the glasses and handed Kanati one. "Just never thought it would come through you."

"Me either." He shrugged.

"So why?" He took a large sip. "Why do all of this if you don't have to? I'm confused, Kanati. This is way out of your personality."

"First off you don't know me. You never did. I showed you what I wanted you to see. That's it. Law destroyed everything I had," Kanati said. "And he killed my grams, my brother and my friend. That's why I don't give a fuck about nobody no more."

His jaw dropped. "Impossible."

"Guess there's a lot you don't know about your son."

"That may be true but you are a good person. Don't be like him."

"Look where being a good person got me?" Kanati yelled. "What else I got now?"

"I see hate in your eyes that wasn't there before, Kanati. I mean, are you really ready to give this situation your soul?"

"I already did."

"I wish that weren't true." Kanati drank the rest of the vodka and sat the glass on the counter.

"Just so you know, I know you didn't burn down my house."

"How you find out?" Kanati frowned, already knowing he never committed the act.

"I got the video from a neighbor of mine the other day. The fire department needed it and so did my insurance company to file my claim. After examining them I saw Sunni running around the house with a gasoline canister. I dropped the DVD off where my son was staying a little while ago. So he'll know too."

"Wow, all this for nothing," he said softly.

"Yes. So please don't kill me."

"You know I can't do that." Kanati smiled, having felt vindicated by the truth although it didn't change his moves. "But you wouldn't wanna give me the address to where I can find your son next would you? I wanna go there after."

"You know I can't do that," Jimmy whispered.

Kanati shrugged. "It was worth a try." He took a deep breath. "Now finish that up." He pointed at the glass with the barrel. "It's time to go." He cocked the weapon and aimed.

Jimmy downed all his liquor and then...BOOM!

Brain matter slapped against the kitchen sink behind him.

CHAPTER TWENTY

LAW

Law was peacefully asleep in Vanessa's bed. After grabbing some dinner with his ex-girlfriend and enjoying her conversation he decided against going back to the motel. Because after dealing with Sunni's craziness on the regular, and her abusing herself in the bathroom, coupled with his almost getting killed, he needed a break.

When he opened his eyes Vanessa was standing on the side of the bed with a tray filled with croissants, bacon, eggs and coffee.

"Whoa," he smiled sitting up, his back against the headboard. He inhaled the aroma of the food deeply. "You went all out huh?"

"After the D you gave me last night," she placed the tray over his legs and walked around to the other side of the bed, easing under the covers next to him. "I had to hook you up."

He looked over at her cute face and smiled. Instead of the long red wig she always wore, her natural black hair was pulled in a bun on top of her head. "You know, I forgot how good you felt when I was inside of you. But you sure know how to remind a nigga huh?"

"Well since you remember, maybe this time you won't forget," she winked, grabbed a piece of bacon and nibbled a little.

"Thanks for last night, Vanessa." He was sincere as he looked into her eyes. "I really mean that."

"You don't have to thank me anymore, Law," she said lying on her side. "We friends now." She ate the rest of the bacon in her hand. "And that's what friends do."

"I get that but I'm really starting to believe I made a mistake by letting you go." He paused. "I mean, you were the perfect woman at my side and —"

"I spoke my mind too much."

He laughed. "Yeah, why you do that?"

She playfully punched him in the arm and they both laughed. "Fuck you!"

"No seriously," he said looking into her eyes. "Only a sucker ass nigga would fuck up with you. And that's exactly what I did."

"What you saying now, Law?" She paused. "Because I don't want my heart messed with no more if you act like you want me, only for it to be a lie.

Please don't do that. It would hurt too much and I don't deserve it."

"I wouldn't hurt you again. Ever."

"Good," she said firmly. "Because you think them niggas after you now," she shook her head from left to right. "The last thing you want is me on your naughty list. I'd do way more damage."

"Listen, this is what I want you to know." He put his index finger under her chin and lifted her gaze so that she was looking at him. "I fucked up. And I know I fucked up. So all I'm asking is for some time to get shit right on the streets. And with Sunni. Now I'm not gonna lie, I got a kid on the way and if we do decide to be together you'd have to deal with that."

"Wow…I almost forgot about her being pregnant."

"I know, but if you give me a chance I promise I'll meet you more than halfway. I'll be the man you deserve."

Vanessa looked away. "You mean help you raise an Indian baby with silky, curly, black hair?" She grinned and looked at him again. "You know what, I think I can get with that," she said playfully.

"You stupid." He grabbed a croissant.

"Stupid like this pussy." She lifted the tray and sat it on the far side of the bed, before straddling him. He tossed the croissant across the room to have access to both hands.

"Oh so the pussy stupid now huh?" He said playfully placing one hand on each side of her waist. "So that's why I was laughing last night?"

"Nigga, fuck you," she said play punching him before kissing him passionately. "You mean that's why you were moaning like a bitch last night."

Grabbing her ass cheeks he said, "Somebody look like they up for round two." He tossed her on the bed and slipped inside of her, almost knocking the tray over. "Damnnnnnn, and you still wet."

Vanessa pulled up in front of the motel and took a deep breath. "Are you sure you want me to wait? I can pick you up later if you need a little more time."

Law looked at the motel door. "Nah, I want you to hang out here for a while. She's not gonna want to hear what I'm about to say but I need to be honest. Give me some time and I be right back."

Vanessa looked at him and at the motel. "Law, I want you to know that you don't have to do this for me. I'm happy with just being there for you and with you. Don't rush this situation on account of me."

He sat back. "I'm tired of doing shit the wrong way in life." He sighed deeply. "If we gonna work its gonna be built on no more lies." He looked at the motel and pushed open the door. "I be back." He winked.

Exiting the truck he walked into the motel room using his key card. When he opened the door neither Petey or Sunni were in sight. Trudging to the bathroom he looked inside and again saw no one. Figuring they went to get something to eat he sat on the edge of the bed and called Petey.

"Hey, man, where you at?" He paused. "You got Sunni with you? If so hit me back and let me know if she's okay. Plus I have to talk to her 'bout something she won't like. Later."

Realizing he wasn't going to find out where they were that way he called L.F. instead. For real it had been some time since he'd spoken to him. After Moozy died, L.F. had been a little distant and he figured it was because he was hurt about losing a friend. But truthfully he didn't know what was going on in the man's mind. He wouldn't take his calls.

200 **By T. STYLES**

Picking up the phone he hit him up anyway and surprisingly L.F. answered immediately. "Hey, man, where you at? You okay?"

"I'm at home," L.F. said. "But how you though? For real?"

Law got up and walked toward the window. "I'm at the motel room looking for Petey and Sunni. They not here. You talk to 'em?" He pushed the curtain aside and smiled at Vanessa who was still parked out front and waiting. She blew a kiss when she saw him.

"Nah. Petey hit me the other night about going to grab something to eat." He paused. "But then he called back five minutes later and said you asked him to do something so he couldn't meet up with me. I ain't seen or heard from the nigga since."

"Yeah, Sunni was tripping so I needed him to help me work that out." Law sighed. "We cool now though."

"Man, you sound alright considering everything that's going on."

Law released the curtain and looked down. On the floor was a DVD wrapped in a white paper sleeve marked LAW. He sat on the edge of the bed, picked it up and looked at it. "Considering what?"

"Wait...you don't know?"

Law frowned. "What you talking about, man?"

"Wow," L.F. said. "I really wish this shit didn't fall on me to do but I guess it does." L.F. took a deep breath. "Your pops is dead. Kanati got to him."

Law leapt to his feet. "Fuck you mean?"

"Just what I said. Kanati killed your pops." He paused. "It's been on the news and everything. What you gonna do?"

CHAPTER TWENTY-ONE

KANATI

Kanati woke up to the smell of fresh bacon and pancakes cooking in his kitchen. He smiled because he was supposed to be home alone and once again it appeared that Tammi failed to listen and had come over uninvited.

This time he was grateful for her intrusion because he was hungry as fuck.

Pushing himself out of bed, he wiped his curly hair out of his face and bopped to the kitchen. Standing behind her, he watched as she flipped hotcakes on the stove with precision. Her fat ass showing through her black stretch pants.

She looked back at him and smiled before focusing on breakfast again. Snaking his arms around her waist he kissed her on the cheek. "How the fuck you get in the house?" He asked playfully.

"I copied the key when I found the place for you," she smiled. "You should already know how sneaky I can be."

He thought about her comment and how he always suspected she was holding back on something she wasn't trying to tell him, but he decided to leave it alone. Instead he shook his head and walked to the table, where he was able to look at her work.

He sat down. "I wish things were different." He thought about how shit would feel if this was his life on the regular. "And this was my world."

She placed the last hotcake on the plate with the bacon and walked over to him. "Why you say that?"

"Because the things I've done won't allow me to be happy."

She made their plates and sat next to him. "Kanati, I know you don't feel like you can talk to me."

"It's not that."

"Yes it is and I get it," she placed her hand over his. "I just wish that you let me in somehow. I mean I'm not dumb. I know you here for revenge but I guess I'm just wondering if you're thinking about an end game. You deserve peace, we all do, and I want that peace to be with me."

"That's just it," he paused. "It's too late for me. I've already sold my soul."

Her eyes widened. "What does that mean?" She got up and walked toward him. He moved the chair and pulled her softly onto his lap.

"Listen...I'm gonna make a call tonight." He exhaled deeply. "And if I get the right answer, I'm done out here. No more violence. No more murder."

She looked down at her hands and twiddled her fingers. "So that means you'll be going back home and it's over for us too?"

"How you sound? So you saying you not gonna visit me in Arizona?"

She got up and he pulled her down again onto his lap. "No, I guess what I'm saying is I want more. I mean, I *need* more. So if you want me to move to Arizona I need to know it's permanent. But I'll go with you anywhere."

He took a deep breath. "Listen, I—"

KNOCK. KNOCK. KNOCK.

He shoved her off softly, reached behind him and grabbed his gun. Tammi's eyes widened because she didn't even know he had it on him. Creeping to the door slowly, he pushed the curtain to the side and looked out the window. When he saw who was out front he looked back at her.

"I'm sorry," she said softly. "I was worried that you were alone out here and I couldn't have that."

He shook his head, tucked the gun in his pants and opened the door. Shilah and Micco walked in with their other good friend Easy. After giving Kanati dap, Shilah and Micco walked up to Tammi, kissed her on the cheek and smiled. "Thank you for telling us where he was," Shilah winked at her.

"Now you gotta tell him not to be mad at me," she said softly.

"I'll work on him," Micco said.

"Hey, bae, let me holla at my dudes right quick," Kanati said. "And we gonna talk about this later."

She nodded and walked toward the back of the house like a two-year old in trouble.

Kanati took a deep breath, flopped on the sofa and ran his hands down his jeans. Leaning back he said, "What's up?"

"That's all you got to say to us, nigga?" Micco asked, glaring down at him. "Are you fucking crazy or something? Out here on the solo?"

Kanati ran his hands down his face. "I mean, what you want me to say?"

"We want you to tell us why you leave without letting us know where you were going?" Micco continued. "When we were in Arizona! And then didn't tell us how to find you. Thank God for Tammi because you had us fucked up in the head!"

"Man, I did that because I knew you would come back with me." He paused. "And I wanted to finish this thing on my own."

"But we started it together," Micco snapped. "And this not the way you do niggas you say you fuck with."

"I get that," Kanati said looking down trying to push away the guilt. "But your moms just died, we buried Bid and you were under a lot of pressure so—"

"My moms just died and now I'm supposed to stay out there and lose a brother too back in Baltimore?" Micco persisted. "Nah, fuck that."

Kanati nodded. "So now you bring Easy in all this mess?"

"Shit, I woulda came a long time ago had I known ya'll was getting it in out here," Easy said folding his arms over his chest. "But after what they did to Bid and my mama's house, it wasn't even up for negotiation. I had to help out the home team."

"So what's the plan?" Shilah asked Kanati.

Kanati took a deep breath. "That's just it." He nodded. "I'm gonna hit this nigga up and see where my grandmother is. If she's alive I'm taking her and we going home. That's on my life."

"You think they'll give her up now?" Micco asked.

"I'm not even sure, man," Kanati said. "I took out Law's father last night."

Shilah's eyes widened. "What the fuck?" He yelled. "That was supposed to be last resort shit! We discussed it!"

"Well I was tired of playing games." Kanati shrugged. "Was tired of waiting too."

Shilah walked away and came back. "Man, this not going to end the way I wanted. It's about to — "

RING. RING. RING.

Kanati looked at his new cell phone on the wooden living room table and picked it up. It was a phone number he didn't recognize. Pressing the answer button he said, "Who this?" He quickly placed it on speaker.

"You didn't have to do that," Law said. It was apparent that he had been crying because his throat sounded wet. "My father was always good to you."

Kanati looked at his friends who crowded around the phone, each with a scowl on their faces as if they could see Law's face on the screen. "You started this war." Kanati corrected him. "And you can end it by letting my grandmother go. Is she — "

"Kanati, how are you," Nanni said in her native language suddenly appearing on the line.

Kanati leapt up. "Nanni, are you...you...are you..."

"I'm fine."

Pacing wildly he could hardly keep the phone from shaking. It was Shilah who removed it from his hand and held it for his friend.

"And I want you to know that I love you, Kanati." Nanni continued in their native tongue. "Very, very much. And I've had another dream and in it you—"

"Nanni, I'm coming for you!" He said interrupting her, afraid of hearing another scary prophesy. "I promise you."

"Kanati, it's my time, son. My life is over. I want—"

Suddenly they heard gurgling noises and the call went silent. Each man present could feel her soul leaving this world.

Kanati yelled and turned away.

"You know the funny part, man." Law paused. "I was gonna let it go but you had to fuck with my pops. Why you do that?"

Kanati, with quickened breaths walked back up to the phone and said, "Everything you know is about to die. Get ready."

CHAPTER TWENTY-TWO

LAW

Law sat on the back porch of Vanessa's house and looked out into the yard. The luscious color of her grass for some reason gave him peace. She didn't have a stitch of furniture out back and because of it the lawn was natural. Untouched. Nothing like his life.

When the door opened and she sat next to him, handing him a cup of tea, he sipped it and said, "Fuck is this?"

"Chamomile."

"Cham-omill what?"

"Just drink it, Law," she said. "It'll help calm your nerves a little. And trust me you need it."

He sighed and sat the cup on the step at his feet. "Can't nothing calm me down right now." He looked outward. "I'm on some other shit you hear me?"

She nodded. "Any word yet?"

"Nope. My uncles and them said he was cremated. Nobody wanted to go to the funeral because word got out that somebody would shoot everybody in attendance." He shrugged. "It's like...my pops didn't deserve this type of shit you know?"

She nodded. "Yeah. I agree. I definitely fucked with him." She sighed. "So what now?"

"I'm meeting with some dudes I used to roll with and L.F. later tonight. I got to find this dude, Vanessa. I can't be moving like this out here. Hiding in hovels like a fucking rat." He paused. "Then niggas telling me that he probably got Petey and Sunni and just not telling me." He paused. "I wish I never —"

"Nope, we not doing that anymore," she said cutting him off.

"Doing what?"

"Saying what we wish would've happened or not happened." She picked up the tea and took a sip. "What we have to do now is be smarter than ever." She looked outward, at the horizon.

He sighed. "But how do you strategize when you don't know his next move? This nigga is hiding in my city, like he been here all the time."

"Maybe you should meet up with the dude Tone."

He shook his head no from left to right. "Nah, can't do that."

"Why?"

"Because even though he put the bounty on Kanati's head for what he did on the streets, he still blames me for it. Said I should've never let him come to the city to begin with. Fucking up his money and what not."

"Listen, you can't go to war alone, Law." She placed the cup down on the lower step and scooted closer to him. "Now I don't like that things have gone this far. And for real I could've never imagined that Kanati would be this dangerous but he is."

"Yeah, he too fine to be doing something like this," Law said sarcastically, mocking her voice. "Ain't that what you said?"

She giggled. "Yeah, yeah, yeah, I said that before you were my boyfriend, again." She paused and nudged him with her shoulder. "I did like how he looked but that doesn't mean I don't want him to get everything he deserves."

He rolled his eyes. "Yeah whatever."

"Listen, I did think Kanati was fine but he also fucked with somebody I care about. And although I didn't want things going further than they already have I do believe that we can put an end to this. He in our city not the other way around." She touched his hand. "So go to Tone. It's time for Baltimore niggas to rise up."

Law, L.F. and Vanessa stood in front of Tone who was sitting in an old underground museum in Baltimore city. Back in the day it was used to show visitors slave artifacts from the 1800's but now it was forgotten and abandoned.

Tone was sitting on a high back hardwood chair with five men behind him. All were armed and hated Law Hightower with a passion.

"Nobody eats until Law Hightower is six feet deep," Tone chanted. "Ain't that's what they saying out there?"

Law rolled his eyes.

"I lost ten good niggas because of you," Tone said pointing at him with a long finger. "Dudes who made me a lot of money. A few top men I know lost even more."

On some attitude shit Law said, "Look, I ain't the one who—" Vanessa placed her hand softly on Law's arm to silence him. Taking the hint, Law took a deep breath and raised his chin. "I'm listening."

"Are you, lil nigga?" He frowned. "Because it don't look like it to me."

Law nodded. "I said I'm listening."

Tone stood up. "So tell me why I shouldn't kill you right now and be done with it once and for all? Because the way I see it, if you die today I get my blocks back."

"Because its time to stand together," Law said softly. "Yeah I made some wrong moves, but what he doing now is fucked up on all levels. This ain't Arizona! This Baltimore! Kanati brought niggas into the fight who ain't have nothing to do with our shit when he murdered working trap men. Killed my father, took my baby's mother and even got Petey!"

"Is it true?" Tone asked, gritting his teeth.

"Is what true?"

"That all this shit started for her?" He asked looking at Vanessa before moving closer.

When he was near enough Law placed a firm hand on Tone's chest to stop him from progressing. "Nah, this the one I let get away. Not that bitch Sunni." Tone looked down at Law's hand and Law removed it. "Listen, man, all we want is to put this nigga away. And I'm here because I was hoping we could work together to do that." He paused. "So can we or not?"

CHAPTER TWENTY-THREE

KANATI

Kanati, Shilah, Micco and Easy were sitting at the table in his house going over their plans for the morning. After his grandmother was murdered on the phone, Kanati was eager to move to the next level and that meant annihilation of everybody Law knew.

"Where does Petey live?" Shilah asked him.

"That's the only person who's house I never went to with Jimmy." He sighed. "I know where L.F. lives but I'm sure he playing it smart now and staying off the grid and out of his house. He—"

Suddenly a blood-curdling scream within the house rocked all of them onto their feet. Kanati ran to the back, into his bedroom, only to see Tammi on the floor crying. He rushed up to her while his men checked the windows to see if anyone was outside. When they made sure the coast was clear they remained on guard, eager to find out what was going on.

"What's wrong?" Kanati asked on his knees with her. "You hurt?"

"They took my son!" She cried and looked up at him. "Someone took my son from school!"

Kanati rose to his feet and backed up against the wall. As far as he knew she wasn't a mother. So what was she saying now?

And still, this revelation explained everything suddenly, including the secret texting and conversations she had on the phone. "Your son? Fuck is you saying to me, Tammi? You said you didn't have a kid. I asked and you said you didn't have a kid!"

Kanati and Tammi stood in the lobby of Mary Jane's Preparatory School in Baltimore city. It was a private institution, which specialized, in advanced education for babies all the way up to elementary, believing that the early years were the most influential. Most of the children attending were already fluent in two languages one being English and the other Spanish.

"Ma'am, I am so sorry for the confusion I caused," Mrs. Lester said. She was responsible for checking in all visitors and parents. "Someone came to pick up their child and one of our helpers gave them the wrong kid."

"But how is that possible?" She wiped her tears away roughly with the back of her hand.

"I don't know, ma'am," she said apologetically. "I wish I did. But we're getting to the bottom of it now. The good thing is that he's safe and sound." She paused. "Let me go get Austin." She walked away.

Tammi placed her hands in her face and cried. Saddened to see her in such grief, Kanati walked up to her, pulled her into his chest and held her tightly. It was the kind of hug that only a strong man who loved the woman in his arms could muster.

Tammi, sobbed harder. "I thought he was gone." She looked up at him. "I thought he was gone."

"It's gonna be 'aight. They got lil man and that's all you should care about now. Everything gonna be good. I promise."

Five minutes later the cutest little boy who ever walked the earth strutted out. His eyes were wide like black marbles and his smile was infectious. At seven years old Kanati liked him before he even said a word. What was also surprising was that he looked just like Kanati when he was a kid.

VILLAINS: IT'S SAVAGE SEASON 217

He was wearing a blue Star Wars backpack and holding a yellow piece of construction paper with a brown pyramid pasted on it. He seemed to be proud of his work and showcased it like it was an award.

Elated, Tammi bent down and picked him up, squeezing him into her arms. "Mommy, what's wrong?" He said noticing her sadness. "You like my picture? I made it for you."

She placed him down, removed it from his hands and looked at it. Wiping the tears from her face she tried to examine it with love. To say she was relieved and filled with joy that her little boy was okay was an understatement. "It's perfect, Austin! You did such an amazing job! I'm gonna put it right on the wall at home!"

"Then why you crying?" He asked in a sad voice.

"Because she misses you and is happy to see you. That's all, little man." Kanati said, rubbing his bushy coal black curly hair.

"You look like daddy!" He said smiling brightly. He'd seen a picture once and they favored. "Is he daddy, mommy?"

Kanati took one step back and placed his hands into his pockets before crossing his arms over his chest. *That was strange.* He thought. Did Tammi have a

By T. STYLES

particular type of dude? There were so many questions and yet the things he had going on in his life didn't allow for the answers. "Oh yeah?" Kanati said to the little boy.

"Yep!" Austin said excitedly before jumping up and down. "You look like daddy, you look like daddy," he continued to sing.

Now things were beyond awkward.

"Come on, silly," Tammi said to him. "Let's take you to grandma's house."

KANATI

When Austin was down for his nap Tammi walked up to Kanati who was in the kitchen talking to her grandmother. She was a delightful woman who was wise and knew a lot about life. He felt comfortable in her presence and sad at the same time because she reminded him so much of Nanni.

"I'll leave you two alone now," she said touching Kanati on the shoulder. "It was nice meeting you, handsome." Turning her attention to her grandchild she kissed Tammi on the cheek and walked out.

Tammi took a deep breath and leaned against the refrigerator. "Today was crazy right?"

"Why you fucking lie to me?" He asked walking up to her. He waited for that exact moment when they were alone and the kid was safe to step to her about her deceit. "I'm not understanding this shit, Tammi." He said through clenched teeth. "I was falling for you and you lied."

"About what?"

He stared at her.

With guilt, she looked down and took a deep breath. "I know you're mad but I wanted to be honest. And I'll be honest now."

"Oh now you wanna be honest?" Kanati said with a scowl. "You been lying to me from the gate. Why should I trust anything you say?"

"I know I lied and I'm so sorry." She sniffled. "It's just that my son's school is expensive, Kanati. And I was worried that when you asked if I had any kids that you wouldn't give me the job. I needed the money." She paused and wiped the tears creeping up on her cheeks away. "And I knew you hated kids so—"

"I don't hate kids." He waved the air. "You sound silly."

"Then why you didn't want me to have any?"

"Because I'm a hood nigga. Out here on some serious shit." He said louder than he wanted. "And I would never have gotten you mixed up in half the things I had going on had I known you were a mother. Why would I want your son to be missing his moms like I missed mine? Huh?"

"But—"

"I can't have you around me anymore." He interrupted. "Your kid needs you to be here for him and I got niggas after me." He pointed at the floor. "Don't you get that?"

"Kanati, please don't do this," she said wrapping her arms around him tightly, trying to stop him from leaving. "I need you and—"

"Quit!" Kanati yelled, shoving her backwards. "I gotta go."

"Kanati, I'm begging—"

Glass from the window behind her came shattering toward them. It was as if it were in slow motion and Kanati, thinking on his feet, knocked her down to the floor. With her out the way, he released the hammer from his waist and fired back at the broken window.

Unfettering shot after shot, he moved toward the window and busted off until he heard tires peeling away from the scene.

"Tammi, you alright?" He asked walking up to where he laid her down. When he looked down he saw Tammi reaching up for him, her mouth filled with blood. "K...Kanati...help." Her hand extended upwards to him, fingers crimson red. "I can't...I can't breathe."

CHAPTER TWENTY-FOUR

KANATI

Kanati was in the waiting room at the hospital, a nervous ball of Navaho Indian mess. Shilah, Micco and Easy were also with him to lend support and protection. All three were strapped and looked up every so often; especially when the elevator opened and someone stepped out.

They had all intentions on being respectful to the sick but if drama happened they would unleash war like no one had ever seen. There was a slight reason that Kanati was at a little ease. As far as they knew the cops didn't mention Tammi's injury in the news for fear that whomever did the crime would come back to finish the job.

"You know the thing with her kid being snatched was so they could follow you to her house right?" Shilah asked, sitting next to Kanati. "They snatched him knowing it would lead to you. And it worked."

Kanati took a deep breath. "Yeah. I figured it out too. 'Cept it was too late by then."

"Man, I want this nigga Law dead," Micco said standing up as if the seat were on fire.

"What you about to do?" Shilah asked Micco, sensing his agitation.

"Me and Easy 'bout to keep an eye out in the front of the hospital to make sure they don't pull up on us." Micco exhaled. "I'm not letting them hit anybody else on our watch." Micco and Easy stormed off.

Kanati sighed. "Fuck." He rubbed his palms down his jeans.

Shilah placed a hand on his shoulder. "We can always get on that plane and lay low for awhile." He paused. "And then come back to do shit the right way."

He frowned, his brows lowered. "You know that's not happening now, Shi. You do understand that right?" He looked at him. "There's no way I'm leaving her alone, man." He pointed outward. "Not like this."

Shilah nodded. "I knew you would say that."

Kanati sighed. "But what I want to know is what the fuck she lie for?" He asked passionately. "I would've never had her involved had I known she had a son. You should see that little kid. I'm just happy he's safe."

"She's in love with you." He paused. "And she knew that was a deal breaker."

"I love her too but—"

"Whoa." Shilah said sitting up.

"What?"

"I never heard you say you loved a woman." Shilah smiled. "Ever." He paused. "But for once I can say I approve. Tammi is funny, beautiful but more than anything she was willing to put her life on the line to be with you. Can't get much more dedicated than that can you?"

Kanati sighed. "Guess I didn't know I loved her until now." He stood up and paced a little. "Except now she may...she may die and—"

"Let's not expect the worse just yet, man." Shilah said cutting him off. "We don't know what may happen. Plus you deserve a break in life. Let's hope you get it with her."

Kanati nodded. "We have to do something, Shi. I can't wait around here for something else to pop off."

"Then what we waiting on?"

LAW

Law, L.F. and James, one of their other friends were in the middle of Vanessa's living room smoking, drinking and boasting. After successfully drawing Kanati out of his hole, they were excited about killing Tammi, or so they thought. Although sad originally that they couldn't hit Kanati, now they were relishing the progress.

"I know that nigga fucked up now!" Law said excitedly. "Taking out his bitch is just the beginning though." He pointed at them. "We gotta do more."

"You should've hit the kid too!" L.F. said. "We would've made our presence known then."

"Shut the fuck up with all that noise," Law snapped. "That wasn't the point of going out there. Ain't nobody—"

"The kid?" Vanessa said cutting Law off. She had walked up behind them and they thought they were alone. "You shot up the house with the kid home?" She asked.

"Bae, I—"

"Nigga, fuck you!" Vanessa took off running toward the back of the house. "I can't believe this shit!"

Law looked at L.F. "Thanks a lot, nigga." Afterwards he moved toward the back of the house to go after her. When he made it to the bedroom Vanessa was sitting on the edge of the bed with her arms crossed so tightly over her chest she could've severed her torso. He closed the door behind him and sat next to her.

"What is wrong with you, Law?" She dropped her arms as her right leg jiggled rapidly. "Why would you risk killing a child?"

"What you mean?" He shrugged. "You knew shit could get heated." He paused. "I mean I don't think they hit the kid but—"

"How do you fuckin' know what they did?" She yelled standing up. "You gave orders to fire the house up with the baby inside? What kind of monster are you?"

"Sit down, Vanessa." His temples throbbed. "Stop all that noise."

"No."

"SIT THE FUCK DOWN!" He yelled. Slowly she took a seat and crossed her arms over her chest again. He took a deep breath. "I know this messed up because a kid coulda got killed but Kanati off'd my father, V. I had to take a strong stance against this dude."

"And you did that when you killed his grandmother." She paused. "The plan was to get Kanati! Never the little boy or anybody else."

VILLAINS: IT'S SAVAGE SEASON 227

"But he started it."

"No! You started it!" She yelled pointing at him. "If that baby would've gotten killed I would never have been able to live with myself. Ever!"

"What you talking about?" He yelled. "You act like you pulled the trigger or something. This was all on me."

"But I'm the one who found out who the girl was based on how Tone described her and the van she was driving. Had I not known her they wouldn't have been able to go to her house and almost kill her son."

"Vanessa, stop being over dramatic. Calm the fuck—"

"You promised to wait until she was alone and snatch her." She paused. "Not shoot up her house with her son home, Law. You can get mad and huff all you want but that was the deal."

He stood up. "Listen, the damage is done."

"Is it?"

He shrugged. "I mean what you want me to say?"

She nodded. "You know what, I really believed you could change and now I'm realizing you can't." She sighed. "You still gonna be the same selfish ass nigga you were when I met you in high school. The only thing that's different is your age."

"Bitch, fuck you!"

"Nah! Fuck you and get out my house." She pointed behind him. "Now, Law!"

"Man, I'm not going no where." He turned to walk back into the living room when she followed him aggressively. With Kanati out on the streets he needed her house as a haven. No way he was leaving no matter what she said. She could suck his dick first.

"I want you out of my house, Law!" She yelled behind his neck. "I'm dead serious."

When L.F. and James saw her angry red face they frowned. "What's going on with your girl?" L.F. laughed. "She doing a lot right now. She could never talk to me the way she going at you."

"All of yah get the fuck out!" She continued to scream after being bombarded with disrespect. "Now!"

"You know what..." Embarrassed, Law turned around and stole her in the mouth. The fatty tissue of her lip split open and blood spewed everywhere. Due to the impact of the blow, Vanessa dropped to the floor and held her mouth. He immediately was racked with guilt.

Just like his love for the streets had him running across the country to get a woman that belonged to another had gone horribly wrong, so did his allowing L.F. to rustle him up, causing him to hit his girl.

"I'm sorry, V. I didn't mean to—"

"Fuck you!" She yelled, running toward the back of the house, slamming the door behind her. "FUCK YOU!"

Law ran into the liquor store to buy some vodka, cups and ice. His bad luck with women seemed to know no boundaries and he needed relief. He just hoped the spirits and weed L.F. was rolling in the car would get him some kind of peace.

After leaving the store, and with his paper bag in hand, he slipped into the backseat of L.F.'s car, sitting directly behind him. "Where James at?" He asked since he wasn't in the passenger seat. "He still ain't come back from talking to that bitch yet?" He rifled through his bag and twisted the cap off the vodka. Grabbing a plastic cup he poured a heaping amount, dropped in a few cubes of ice and extended it to L.F. "Here you go. Drink up."

By T. STYLES

Silence.

"L.F.," Law laughed. "Stop fucking around before you don't get shit."

Silence.

"L.F.," Law shoved him in the back and his face fell forward, his forehead pressing against the horn causing it to sound off. Dropping the vodka and cups on the floor he opened the door, got out and pulled open L.F.'s door.

And there he was. Sitting in the front seat with a bullet hole on the side of his head.

The events leading up to his demise were amazing really.

On some serendipitous shit, Kanati happened to be driving down the street and recognized the black Benz from when he was supposed to kill him at his house. Using the opportunity of L.F. not being aware of his surroundings, due to rolling a blunt, he shot him in the side of his temple and dipped back in his car before taking off.

Seeing this from a far, James kicked rocks too.

Thereby saving himself.

It was now Law's move.

Except Kanati wasn't done.

CHAPTER TWENTY-FIVE

KANATI

Dressed in black hoodies and black jeans, their faces were concealed as Kanati, Shilah, Micco and Easy walked into Jimmy's strip club. Finding the perfect spot, they laid claim on an empty section in the back, where they could observe it all. A few customers noticed the odd bunch but when Big Yellow and Big Cocoa, a duo, came out to perform, the strange men were suddenly forgotten.

Grabbing the silver rail at the top of the ceiling, Big Yellow held her body weight, her legs dangling under her. Although lean as a snake, with the exception of her thick ass, she was definitely cock strong. This was proven when Big Cocoa, whose skin was milky chocolate, grabbed the rail in front of her, wrapped her legs around Big Yellow's waist and then released her hold, hanging solely onto Big Yellow by her hips.

Loving the exploit, dollar bills rained from the sky like a hurricane and the crowd went wild. And still, in the back of the establishment, a group of men whose blood ran with Navajo Indian were anything but enthused.

Rising to their feet they unleashed a hail of bullets into the crowd of men and women like maniacs. At one time vowing never to harm females, Kanati temporarily abandoned his morals in Tammi's honor. After all, the love of his life was in a hospital fighting for her existence and as far as he was concerned the rest could suck his big dick.

Empty shells clinked against the hardwood floors as bullets met their hosts. Some people made it out alive. Most didn't. And Kanati could give a fuck less.

When Big Cocoa saw an exit opportunity she took off running toward the back of the club but Kanati caught up with her, grabbing her by her hair he stopped her motions. "I got some questions and for your sake you better have the answers."

Kanati, Shilah, Micco and Easy stood in front of Big Cocoa as she sat bare ass in an alley some ways away from the club. After wreaking havoc in Jimmy's they figured it was best to change scenes. "I don't wanna hurt you," Kanati said softly looking down at her. "So make it easier by telling me what I need to know."

"Of course, anything," she said nodding her head quickly up and down. "I know who you are and I'll tell you anything. You're the villains right?"

Kanati and his friends looked at one another and back at her, tripping out on the tag they had been given.

"We'll be all that," Micco said.

"Law dealt with a female." Kanati said calmly. "Long red hair and —"

"Vanessa!" She blurted out.

Kanati looked back at his friends and then back at her. "That's her name." He said now remembering when she cornrowed his hair; the day Law invited him to that party. "Where is she?"

"I don't know," she cried, black mascara running down her cheeks. "I mean she came by every now and —"

Micco hit her in the mouth with a closed fist, causing blood to drip-drop from her lips. Thereby living up to the Villains officially.

"Please," Kanati said, softly, as if she weren't just struck. "Don't make us do that again. Where is she?"

With tears running down her cheek she lowered her head. "You know, I heard about you," she said in a low voice. "From people around the club. When everything first happened…long before the rapes."

"We didn't rape anybody," Kanati glared.

"I know." She wiped her tears away and her bloody mouth next. "But still, with all the things they said about you I guess they got it wrong."

"Meaning?"

"You do abuse women."

He frowned. "Abuse women?"

She nodded yes and gazed at Micco who cleared his throat.

His ego was damaged a little but he took a deep breath to save face. "Where does she live?" Kanati crossed his arms over his chest. "I won't ask you again."

"Last I heard she had a house in Baltimore County. But it was run down and needed a lot of work. That was a few years ago so things may be different now."

Kanati took a deep breath. "Good. Give me the location." Vanessa told him everything she knew. And when she was done he reached into his pocket and tossed her some money. A fifty swam in a puddle of piss and water nearby. "Get yourself a ride out of here, 'fore one of these niggas do rape you."

They were about to walk away when she said, "I wish I met you before all this happened and you turned out like this. Maybe I could've saved you."

He laughed. "Save yourself first. You playing yourself like a whore."

Vanessa rolled over in her bed, her mouth throbbing and swollen. She couldn't believe she had gotten involved with Law again and yet she couldn't help but admit that she still loved him.

When she opened her eyes she almost jumped out her skin when she saw Kanati sitting on the bed with no shirt, just jeans. He had taken off the hoodie he wore the previous night and was about to borrow another shirt from her crib. But first he had some questions to ask.

And since there was a possibility that he would kill her and get bloody, he figured changing into a fresh shirt could wait.

"Kanati!" She popped up. "What...what are you doing here?"

"Where is he?" He asked calmly.

"How did you get into my house?"

"Answer the fuckin' question, bitch!" Micco yelled from the right.

It was at that time that she turned her head only to see Micco, Shilah and Easy glaring at her, all holding guns aimed in her direction. "Please, don't hurt me." She begged Kanati." I didn't have anything to do with what happened to your girlfriend."

"And yet you know why I'm here." Kanati responded. "Without my even having to say a word."

She looked down and scooted to her headboard. Pulling the covers over her body she took a deep breath and tried to snake her hands under the pillow, which concealed her .22 handgun.

"It ain't there, ma," Shilah said taking it out of his pocket and waving it. "You might as well tell us what we came for or get fucked up." He tucked it back into his smallest pocket.

She took a deep breath. "He's in jail."

Kanati looked at his crew who all broke out into laughter, feeling the woman was lying at best. Kanati however remained stoned face. "What you mean in jail?"

She took a deep breath. "He hit me in the face and I pressed charges." She poked her bottom lip out for emphasis. "I know I was on some snitch shit when I did it but still." She shrugged. "I can't have no nigga hitting on me." She sighed. "While he was in there I also told them about the shootout at Tammi's house."

"Wait, so you serious?" Shilah asked stepping closer.

She nodded yes.

Kanati stood up and walked to the window in her room. The sun gleamed against his face. If this was true he had many issues at the moment. For starters this wasn't how he wanted Law and his destiny to end. He spent so much time obsessing about revenge that he never thought for once that the universe would get in the mix and change the course of his plans.

Kanati looked at Shilah. "Find out if she's telling the truth."

"I'm on it." Shilah removed his cell phone from his pocket and bopped out the room.

Vanessa gazed at Kanati. She noticed he looked so angry and wore a permanent scowl. "Do you remember when I asked why you smile so much?"

Kanati searched his mind but couldn't remember smiling recently, let alone talking to her. "Nah."

Her eyes widened. "Kanati, it was the night we came into the house you were living in at Jimmy's place. I sat next to you on the sofa. We were going to a party and—"

"I don't remember, Vanessa," Kanati said, slightly irritated by her goofy recollection. So much violence had happened that his mind erased every light moment, replacing it with thoughts of bodies dropping, tissue ripping and blood pouring.

"Wow, we really fucked you up mentally didn't we?" She asked sadly.

Silence.

"Anyway, I asked you why you smile so much and you said it helps to keep the rage away." She paused. "I always knew something dark was sitting at the surface, waiting to be released and now I know what it was. Hate."

"She's telling the truth," Shilah said reentering the room. "He's locked up."

"Wow," Kanati said shaking his head. He walked to the closet and grabbed a fresh t-shirt and a grey hoodie that belonged to Law, from hangers. He had gone shopping a few days before they came. "Where are Petey and Sunni?"

"I don't know, Kanati. I swear to God. We thought you killed them." She paused. "And Law was looking for them after watching the DVD."

"What DVD?"

"The DVD of Sunni burning down his father's house," she paused. "He wanted to lay hands on her because all of this drama came from that one act. The way Law was carrying on I think he was gonna kill her himself."

"This didn't happen because of her burning down the crib," Kanati corrected her. "This happened because niggas ain't satisfied with what's in their own yard. And they gotta rummage through other people's shit. This is all about greed, ma. Nothing less. Nothing more."

"Are you...I mean...are you gonna kill me now?" She asked, fearing the worst.

"Nah."

She exhaled, relieved.

They all moved toward the door and Kanati realized there was a lot to think about. Maybe he should go back home after making sure Tammi was okay. He was really considering letting the matter go until Vanessa said, "She's pregnant."

Kanati turned around and looked down at her. "What you just say?"

"Sunni's pregnant...with Law's child. In case you wanted to know."

CHAPTER TWENTY-SIX

KANATI

When Kanati sauntered into the hospital room wearing an old man's jacket, a grey mustache and his hair pushed up in a bucket hat, he pulled it all off when he saw Tammi lying in bed with her eyes open. He never expected her to be conscious this soon but now he had renewed hope for her health.

Rushing up to her bedside he gripped her hand and said, "Baby, I'm so fucking sorry."

She smiled at him. "So this is what you meant when you said you didn't want me involved?"

He laughed. "Had I known I would've—"

"This isn't your fault, Kanati. This was on me. When a person gives you a warning and you don't heed it, you don't have nobody to blame but yourself." She smiled. "I love you, Kanati." She said with all her heart. "And I don't want you feeling guilt because of this."

"But how can I not?"

"On the first day you met me I lied," she shrugged. "And now I got bullets in my body to show for it. But guess what, I'm alive." Her eyes widened. "Oh wait, they did take the bullets out right?" She touched her chest.

He smiled. "Yeah."

She exhaled and stared at him for what seemed like forever. "You are so fine when you smile."

"So you in the hospital talking about how I look now?" He chuckled.

"Yep. And if I could flash you my boobs I would but this hospital gown too long."

He lowered his body and kissed her gently on the lips. She used the opportunity to grab a handful of his hair and inhale. It smelled like shampoo. "Don't leave me, Kanati." She released him and stared into his eyes. "Please."

He rose, pulled a chair next to the bed and sat down by her. "I can't tell you what I'm gonna do right now." He paused. "But the only thing on my mind is making sure you're okay."

"My body is okay but what about my heart?"

"Tammi." He sighed.

"Seriously." She said with wide eyes. "If you leave I don't know if I'll pull through. I might still die."

He smirked. "You in here cracking jokes, threatening to flash me and talking in full sentences. This all after you got lit up with bullets in your chest.

I'm not a betting man but I feel confident in saying you gonna be 'aight."

"Kanati, please."

He took a deep breath. "My grandmother use to say something to me when she was alive." He paused and looked down at their hands, which were clasped together. "She said man's biggest mistake is not realizing how precious *now* is. How precious the *present moment* is. She said we spend every second thinking about the past or future and that we never just sit back and be grateful. I'm doing that now. With you."

"What does that mean?" She asked as tears rolled down her cheek thinking he was about to catch the first flight across the country.

"It means right now that there is nothing more important to me than being with you right here. And it means that I'm in love with you."

She exhaled deeply. It was the first time he uttered the words and her knees were weak. Good thing she was laying down. "Wow, I didn't think I would ever —"

"What I just say about the past?"

She smiled. "I know it just feels so good to hear you love me."

"Then say that," he lowered his body and kissed her lips again.

She exhaled, glanced at the TV and back at him. "If you could have the perfect life what would it look like?"

He thought about it and sighed deeply. "I don't know if it's possible to have a *perfect* anything. I think I was bored with life and got a whole lot of it at one time...with this war. So I just want to wake up knowing that I'm a man of my word. Knowing that the people in my world can genuinely count on me and that I'm loved."

"Well you know you need me to make that complete right?" She smiled.

"You don't quit do you?"

She laughed harder.

"Austin said I looked like his father." Kanati remembered. "Is that true?"

She smiled and turned away.

"Well?" He continued.

She looked at him. "Yes." Her smile disappeared. "It's kind of gross actually. I was at a family reunion many years ago. And I didn't want to go because I don't know about your people, but something always seems to happen when mine get together. Well," she

VILLAINS: IT'S SAVAGE SEASON   245

sighed, "I sat out in the parking lot of the recreation center thinking, why should I waste any of my time on this? Just because we family don't mean I should let them get on my nerves."

"So did you go inside?"

"Nope. And it was then that Chris walked up to the car and looked over at me. That's Austin's father. You guys look so much a like you could be brothers. " She shook her head. "Anyway, the first thing he said was, *'You not going in are you? I can tell by the look on your face.'* I said, *'Nope'*. He said, *'Wanna get out of here?'* I said, *'Yep'*. The next thing I know we in a motel room eating pizza and watching back to back episodes of the *Golden Girls*."

"Was this dude related?" Kanati frowned, fearing incest.

"Said he wasn't."

"Was he?"

"Yes and no." She paused. "He ended up being the husband of a long distance cousin of mine. I guess he was angry that she was divorcing him later that week. To get back at her he came uninvited and found me...the perfect revenge. His plan was to let her know that he fucked a family member but there were two problems. One was I wasn't aware of this plot and the second I was fertile at the time."

"Whoa." He wiped his hand down his face.

"I kept the baby and everybody in my family hated me for it too." She paused. "Even my grandmother found it hard to look into my eyes in the beginning. But once Austin got here even she couldn't deny him. Kanati, he's filled with so much love and even though his father declined to be in his life I can truly say he's a happy little boy. And I'm glad I didn't abort him like my family wanted."

"What happened with your cousin?"

"Check this shit out, she got back with that nigga!"

"Fuck out of here!"

"Nope. Last I heard they were living in North Carolina and had three more kids, all looking like my son." She shrugged. "They just don't acknowledge Austin which is sad because he wants to be loved so badly."

Kanati looked down at his hands. "Maybe we can—"

"Kanati, we got some info for you," Micco said walking into the room. When he saw Tammi's eyes were opened Micco rushed over to her and kissed her on the forehead. "You a fucking trooper you know that?"

She grinned. "Please take care of him," she said to Micco knowing they were about to leave.

"I got him. Trust me."

Kanati walked up to the bed and kissed her on the lips. "Shit will work out." He placed his fingers over his heart. "I can feel it." He winked at her.

Micco put a firm hand on Kanati's shoulder to remind him it was time to bounce. "Come on, man."

They walked out.

Kanati, Micco, Shilah and Easy stood behind the hospital near the dirty laundry entrance. "So the dude Petey moved to Louisiana, man," Shilah said excitedly. "And get this, niggas are saying he has Sunni with him too."

Kanati scratched his curly hair. "What the fuck?"

"Exactly," Shilah said. "So I figure we should —"

"Go home," Kanati said firmly.

"Come again?" Shilah paused.

"I'm done with everything."

Micco's eyes widened. "So even though you made the vow to kill everything alive, you leaving niggas breathing now?"

"I'm tired of it all, Micco." He raised his hands from his sides and dropped them. "I almost lost my girl and I almost lost you niggas too." He pointed at them. "I'm not letting nobody else die on my watch."

Micco placed his hands on his hips, walked a few feet away and turned his back in his friends' direction. "Wow. I can't believe this shit."

Shilah moved closer to Kanati. "So that means you coming home too right?"

Kanati looked at him. "Nah."

"Wait, so you not coming back either?" Easy asked. "Because when I got the itinerary it said when the war was over everybody left together." He paused. "What part am I missing?"

"I got my girl here, man," Kanati shrugged. "Vulnerable. And until I can make sure shit is safe I can't leave her to the wolves."

Shilah ran his hand down his face. "This is bananas. I don't mean to be insensitive but we still have moves to make."

"I'm sorry, man," Kanati said to him. "I really am."

VILLAINS: IT'S SAVAGE SEASON   249

"It ain't about being sorry!" Shilah yelled. "We lost Bid, your brother and your grandmother behind this war. The least we could do is finish shit off and—"

"That's not what I'm sorry about, man," Kanati repeated. "I'm sorry for causing shit to be this way with you. I mean, you were never the type of dude to move by revenge and I did this to you. For that I'm asking for forgiveness."

Shilah shook his head. He was disgusted by it all.

Micco walked back up to Kanati. "Since I've known you whenever you say you going to do something you do it." He pointed at him. "And you want us to believe you really gonna let Petey and that scandalous bitch breathe? You really want us to believe that even with Law being in prison that you gonna let that shit go too?"

"Yeah, man," Kanati said. "It's over. It's time for niggas to go home."

CHAPTER TWENTY-SEVEN

KANATI

TWO YEARS LATER
BALTIMORE COUNTY

Kanati was sitting on the floor in front of his sofa while Tammi was braiding his hair. She was nine months pregnant and they were excited to learn that in a matter of days she would be having twin boys.

"I don't know this answer," Austin said as he laid next to Kanati on his belly, elbows on the floor and his homework between them. "It's hard."

"You can do it but lets count slow." Kanati said pointing at the addition problem. "You got this, Austin."

"But how?" He asked looking up at him.

"You can use your fingers, little man."

"But people say its dumb."

"Nah, it's not dumb. You can use all the tools God blesses you with," Kanati pawed his head. "Now go to your room and finish that up using your fingers. When you done come back and I'll make sure it's right."

Austin grabbed his paperwork off the floor, got up and walked to his room. Tammi had just finished braiding his hair and his long cornrows ran neatly down his back.

"I love how you are with him," she said. "I know I say that all the time but he really cares about you."

"He's my son." He said. "I love him."

She smiled and looked down at him just as he kissed her inner thigh. "Kanati, can I ask you something?"

"Anything."

"Who was on the phone this morning?"

He sighed deeply. "Nobody you need to worry about."

She exhaled. "In these two years I've seen how you are, Kanati. When you think I'm not looking. I see the sadness in you. The remnants of unfinished business in your eyes. What's going on, baby?" She paused. "Talk to me. Prepare me."

He got up and sat next to her on the sofa. "You my wife now. You got my babies inside you." He touched her belly and stroked in circular motions. "And I'm gonna do all I can to make sure you're safe. All I'm asking now is to respect my moves." He paused. "Can you do that?"

She leaned in and kissed him on the lips. "You already know."

PETEY

Petey and Sunni were entertaining friends in their luxurious home in Houston, Texas. Petey, who was now a local pipe distributor for plumbers in the area, just nailed a major gig. Once finished it would net him well over a million dollars adding to their growing empire. Life was different but safe and he didn't have to worry about the street life.

At least for the moment.

When Petey and Sunni first left Baltimore nobody knew what happened to them. It turned out that when Jimmy was murdered they got word that Kanati and his crew was also coming to the motel to kill them. Originally Petey was going to leave town alone until Sunni begged him to take her along.

There was one problem with her request. He couldn't stand the bitch. He was angry that in his opinion the war started over her and that Law would've been better off if she never entered the picture. But seeing her vulnerability, especially when she got on her knees and kissed his feet, he decided to do something he never thought he would.

Betray a friend.

In an effort to live, they ran around from state to state. First to Louisiana and then Texas. As time went on Petey learned about her painful past. He never knew until they spent night after night in different motels that her uncle had raped her and sold her for profit at a young age. They fell in love by recanting their histories to keep them entertained. He never realized that she spent most of her life being afraid of being alone. He never knew at the core of her was a woman who did not feel like she was good enough, despite her stunning beauty.

Under Petey's firm hand and wise aura Sunni grew to become a more grounded woman. Besides, there was nothing like the threat of being sent back to a world you didn't want to go to calm the ego. And Sunni could see in Law's eyes in that motel room that night that he was officially done with her.

Petey was not only her savior. He was also her last hope. He was her father and her creator.

He may not have been the best looking or tallest man in the world but with her on his arm he was unstoppable. He loved the selfishness out of her soul allowing her to be stronger. And she wanted to be all things to him, genuinely.

In an effort to please him, Sunni taught herself about the pipe business which Petey learned from his father before he died. She lent him a hand wherever she could and made sure when he came home from work meals were prepared for him and Jeremiah, Law's son.

She was the perfect housewife with beauty, smarts and love.

As the years went by they grew more deeply in love than Petey could fathom and in a room full of millionaires, in their half a million dollar home, they felt like the sky was the limit for their lives.

And still, it was all a dream.

After the party was over Petey and Sunni sat on the sofa, exhausted. She smiled at him and leaned in for a kiss. "You are my everything," she said.

"And you are still beautiful." He smiled. "After all these years."

"It's only been two." She giggled, pushing him softly. "I don't age that bad." She looked down at her well-manicured hands. "I can't get over how much I love you, Petey. And yet whenever I think about forever, I remember what Nanni said. That happiness will never truly be mine."

He kissed her again and she rested her head in his lap. "Yeah, it does seem surreal." He played with her long hair, massaging her scalp gently with his fingertips.

"Do you still think it's all temporary?" She asked. "I'm talking about our peace."

Silence.

"Petey?" She looked up at him.

"Yes. It's only for now, Sunni."

A single tear rolled backwards from her eyes upon hearing his answer. Petey had always been wise so why should she doubt him now? "I think that's what makes moments like tonight more special to me." She paused. "There are so many things I would've done differently but—"

"If you had changed one thing, just one, we wouldn't be together now." He paused. "We wouldn't have had the two years and we wouldn't have found real love."

She nodded, knowing like always the words *the wise* Petey uttered were as good as gospel. "So how do you think it will all end?"

"Kanati will take our lives. When we least expect it."

She sighed deeply, having already known the answer. "I wish he would just let us be." She sat up and looked over at him. "I mean, we are the ones who—"

"When I first met him I knew he was different," Petey said cutting her off. "Something about his presence told me he wasn't cut from the same cloth as most dudes. Men with codes honor them above all else. And trust me, Kanati has a code. It's the reason I never wanted this war with him to start. I sensed it at my core. But Law wouldn't listen and now we'll never have everlasting happiness."

She nodded again and eased onto his lap, straddling him. Gazing down at him she said, "Well I will pray for his demise."

He wrapped his arms around her waist. "Never pray for a man's downfall. Pray for our survival."

Death was near.

Before it's presence Petey rested peacefully in bed until he was jolted heavily by the sound of a soft whistle. A whistle that at first may have seemed pleasant and no big deal to the average person. But he heard tale of the sound in the past and knew that to some trap niggas it meant death.

Slowly he pushed the covers back and immediately a thick chill overcame his body. And now that his breath had quickened every time he exhaled, a puff of cold air rolled from his nostrils and floated above before disappearing into the ether.

He hadn't turned the temperature so low so who had?

Whistle.

Startled again, he grabbed the sheet and sat on the edge of the bed. His bare toes pressed into the cool hardwood floor.

Whistle.

With his thoughts choppy, he realized that in his angst he hadn't awakened his beloved to warn her of their fate. But when he reached for Sunni he noticed her space was empty. What was happening?

Slowly he rose and approached the window, the floor creaked softly with his weighty steps. Taking a deep breath, he pushed the thick velvet red curtains to the side and peered out the window. His warm breath caressed the pane, temporarily covering his view with a thick fog. Taking a strong hand he wiped it harshly and what he saw caused him to shiver again.

Standing on the roof of his green Mercedes Benz was Kanati. His long curly hair was tamed at the root with a black bandana but still blew in the wind.

He wasn't alone.

On top of the silver Aston Martin to the right was Shilah and on top of the white Range Rover to the left was Micco.

Holding a knife, Kanati smiled when he saw Petey's face from the window.

"Found you," Kanati yelled. "I hope you made your peace."

When Petey turned around he was knocked down with a blow to the face by Easy.

KANATI

Kanati stood in front of Petey and Sunni who were tied up on chairs in Petey's living room. Behind Kanati were Shilah, Micco and Easy. Although Kanati originally told his friends he had let the matter go, as Shilah knew, his spirit couldn't rest, especially with him having twin boys on the way. He needed to know that all his enemies were gone forever.

"Why the cold air?" Petey asked Kanati, referring to the air conditioner.

Shilah smiled. "I believe you were there when I called Law to bring this to an end," Shilah said. "All I wanted was his grandmother. And it was at that time that I said; *I will stare down at your friends' cold bodies.* Remember now?"

Petey was there and unfortunately he did recall.

Kanati turned his attention toward his ex. "Wow," Kanati nodded examining her expensive pink silk nightgown. "You finally made it." He said looking around. "So tell me this…how does it feel?"

"Kanati," she wept. "Please don't do this."

By T. STYLES

"You know I can't grant any wish of yours. But answer me this," Kanati continued. "Why didn't you just be with Law? And go on with your life? Why did you burn down the house?"

She shook her head. "I was immature but I'm a woman now."

"Congratulations," Shilah said. "But while you were maturing we were left to rebuild our home. The home you never loved." He spit at her feet.

"My grandmother died because of you," Kanati added. "Did you really think I would grant you peace?"

She shook her head slowly from left to right. "What about my son?"

"He'll be fine. I won't let harm come to him." He had plans to call the police and tell them that he was home alone when they were far away.

Kanati looked at them both. "Well." He removed a knife from his back pocket. "Shall we get this shit over with?" He snatched her hair back, exposing her brown neck. Deeply and slowly he slid the blade across her throat, savoring each inch, before she could say a word. When he was done he gave Petey the same ministration and watched as blood poured from their wounds.

VILLAINS: IT'S SAVAGE SEASON

EPILOGUE

Sylvia pulled up in front of the Department Of Corrections and parked when she saw Law waiting with a white plastic bag containing his belongings. A little irritated, he eased into the passenger seat and smiled. "Thanks, Sylvia."

She nodded. "No problem." She pulled off. "Got my money?"

"Really?" He said with an attitude. "You just scooped me up and already you asking about cash?"

"No offense, but you never paid me the last time I cut my finger off." She paused. "Forgive me for not trusting you."

Shaking his head, he reached into the bag, grabbed his wallet and handed her twenty bucks. As she was driving he looked at the missing fingers on her hand that were penned against the steering wheel. "You know, I'm sorry about that shit."

"No problem. Why cry over spilled blood?"

He nodded, thinking her statement was weird. "And I appreciate you picking me up too."

"It's not a problem," she told him pulling into traffic. "I really wanted to do this for you."

By T. STYLES

He nodded.

"But what happened to Vanessa?" She asked. "Why couldn't she come?"

"Fuck that scandalous bitch," he leaned back in his seat. "It's because of her I almost got a lot of time for that shoot-up at Tammi's house. Luckily my lawyer was able to get me only two years though." He looked out the window. "It could've been worse." He sighed deeply. "I don't know why Tammi didn't want to testify but I'm glad she didn't. Because of that I got less time too."

When she reached a red light she looked over at him. "You know what, every night I have pain."

"What you mean?"

"In my hands." She looked at them. "And I always wondered why you never cared. And why you were so cold back in the day."

He looked at her fingers. "Yeah, that's kind of fucked up ain't it?" He paused. "I was a young stupid ass nigga but I'm done now."

"Are you really?" She frowned. "Done now?"

When the light turned green and people began to honk he glared. "Pull off, Sylvia."

She didn't move.

"What you doing?" He looked at her and then back at the road. "Pull the fuck off!"

Silence.

As if he were suddenly struck by lightning his eyes widened and he leaned back. Everything became clear in that one moment. "Wow." He looked down. "Never thought it would end like this but it makes so much sense. Vanessa told me one day you would take your revenge and now—"

She had set him up.

Suddenly two cars pulled up on the right and left and Kanati got out and entered Sylvia's car being sure to sit behind Law, holding him with firm hands to the shoulders. Micco sat behind the driver's seat and Shilah took over behind the wheel when Sylvia slid out.

Law knew his life was over.

When this story ends I'll be a dead man. Law thought.

Don't bother to rush the journey. This isn't some scheme to get you to hear every gory detail of my life either.

Simply put, this is the truth.

My truth.

But if you ask me my biggest regret it's this...I should have never judged the book by its cover the day I met Kanati.

Law sighed. "Don't supposed there's anything I can do to—"

Kanati slammed his hand down on Law's forehead and brought the knife quickly across his neck, tearing into the flesh, fatty tissue, tendons and then bone. When Law was silent neither receiving nor expelling air, he wiped the blade on his shoulder to remove the blood.

Finally, it was done.

Kanati sat in the hospital room holding a baby boy in each arm. Austin stood over him staring at the beautiful babies who were now his brothers.

Looking over at Tammi who was in bed he said, "They are perfect, bae," he smiled harder. "You did good."

"*We* did good." She exhaled as tears rolled down her face. "I can't believe this is my life."

He nodded. "Me either."

She looked at him again and noticed how his face seemed brighter in the recent days that passed. She didn't know what happened a couple of weeks back to warrant his peace but he seemed like a new man.

And for that she was grateful.

"Kanati, why do you smile so much now?"

He looked at her and then focused on his sons. "I smile because I'm happy."

She nodded. "I'm gonna pray that it stays that way."

He winked at her. "Yeah. Me too."

The Cartel Publications Order Form

www.thecartelpublications.com

Inmates **ONLY** receive novels for $10.00 per book.

(Mail Order **MUST** come from inmate directly to receive discount)

Shyt List 1	_____	$15.00
Shyt List 2	_____	$15.00
Shyt List 3	_____	$15.00
Shyt List 4	_____	$15.00
Shyt List 5	_____	$15.00
Pitbulls In A Skirt	_____	$15.00
Pitbulls In A Skirt 2	_____	$15.00
Pitbulls In A Skirt 3	_____	$15.00
Pitbulls In A Skirt 4	_____	$15.00
Pitbulls In A Skirt 5	_____	$15.00
Victoria's Secret	_____	$15.00
Poison 1	_____	$15.00
Poison 2	_____	$15.00
Hell Razor Honeys	_____	$15.00
Hell Razor Honeys 2	_____	$15.00
A Hustler's Son	_____	$15.00
A Hustler's Son 2	_____	$15.00
Black and Ugly	_____	$15.00
Black and Ugly As Ever	_____	$15.00
Year Of The Crackmom	_____	$15.00
Deadheads	_____	$15.00
The Face That Launched A	_____	$15.00
Thousand Bullets		
The Unusual Suspects	_____	$15.00
Ms Wayne & The Queens of DC (LGBT)	_____	$15.00
Paid In Blood	_____	$15.00
Raunchy	_____	$15.00
Raunchy 2	_____	$15.00
Raunchy 3	_____	$15.00
Mad Maxxx	_____	$15.00
Quita's Dayscare Center	_____	$15.00
Quita's Dayscare Center 2	_____	$15.00
Pretty Kings	_____	$15.00
Pretty Kings 2	_____	$15.00
Pretty Kings 3	_____	$15.00
Pretty Kings 4	_____	$15.00
Silence Of The Nine	_____	$15.00
Silence Of The Nine 2	_____	$15.00
Silence Of The Nine 3	_____	$15.00
Prison Throne	_____	$15.00
Drunk & Hot Girls	_____	$15.00
Hersband Material (LGBT)	_____	$15.00
The End: How To Write A	_____	$15.00
Bestselling Novel In 30 Days (Non-Fiction Guide)		
Upscale Kittens	_____	$15.00
Wake & Bake Boys	_____	$15.00
Young & Dumb	_____	$15.00
Young & Dumb 2:	_____	$15.00
Tranny 911 (LGBT)	_____	$15.00
Tranny 911: Dixie's Rise (LGBT)	_____	$15.00

First Comes Love, Then Comes Murder	_____	$15.00
Luxury Tax	_____	$15.00
The Lying King	_____	$15.00
Crazy Kind Of Love	_____	$15.00
Goon	_____	$15.00
And They Call Me God	_____	$15.00
The Ungrateful Bastards	_____	$15.00
Lipstick Dom (LGBT)	_____	$15.00
A School of Dolls (LGBT)	_____	$15.00
Hoetic Justice	_____	$15.00
KALI: Raunchy Relived	_____	$15.00
Skeezers	_____	$15.00
Skeezers 2	_____	$15.00
You Kissed Me, Now I Own You	_____	$15.00
Nefarious	_____	$15.00
Redbone 3: The Rise of The Fold	_____	$15.00
The Fold	_____	$15.00
Clown Niggas	_____	$15.00
The One You Shouldn't Trust	_____	$15.00
The WHORE The Wind		
Blew My Way	_____	$15.00
She Brings The Worst Kind	_____	$15.00
The House That Crack Built	_____	$15.00
The House That Crack Built 2	_____	$15.00
The House That Crack Built 3	_____	$15.00
Level Up (LGBT)	_____	$15.00
Villains: It's Savage Season	_____	$15.00

(**Redbone 1** & **2** are **NOT** Cartel Publications novels and if **ordered** the cost is **FULL** price of $15.00 **each**. **No Exceptions**.)

Please add $5.00 **PER BOOK** for shipping and handling.

The Cartel Publications * P.O. BOX 486 OWINGS MILLS MD 21117

Name: _____

Address: _____

City/State: _____

Contact/Email: _____

Please allow 7-10 BUSINESS days before shipping.

The Cartel Publications is NOT responsible for Prison Orders rejected!

NO RETURNS and NO REFUNDS.

NO PERSONAL CHECKS ACCEPTED
STAMPS NO LONGER ACCEPTED

268   By T. STYLES

CPSIA information can be obtained
at www.ICGtesting.com
Printed in the USA
LVHW110009200519
617758LV00002BB/44/P

9 781945 240256